FICTION WRITING 101

TIPS, TRICKS AND EXERCISES TO GUIDE BEGINNERS IN
FICTION WRITING

BELLEVER BOOKS

CONTENTS

INTRODUCTION

I wasn't unfamiliar with creative writing, even though I'd spent the majority of my teenage years studying music, hoping for a career as a performing songwriter. Learning to play and write instilled in me the discipline and willingness to learn which is part of mastering any skill (much less an art form). And amidst all the rehearsals and practice time, I managed to win a statewide essay competition and get several letters and articles published in various school papers.

It wasn't until I went to Boston's Berklee College of Music that I took a creative writing class (to please my father, if you want to know the truth). The assignment was to identify a pivotal moment in our lives and to write the opening paragraph of its story. The rest of the essay would be completed out of class. I can't recall it exactly, but mine went something like this:

> *I had just turned eighteen and was heading to Boston. I was entering a new phase in my life, and there was one particular burden of childhood I hadn't managed to resolve. It was, and still is, something everybody has to deal with at some point, and it can be a delicate and emotional and sometimes troubling experience. I wanted to do it, about as much as I'd ever wanted to do anything. But I was dreading it. I was nervous. I'd tried before, of course; several times, in fact. And I'd come tantalizingly close. But in the end, the great task had remained beyond me. I just couldn't manage to close the deal. Most of my friends had done it, and I was beginning to feel conspicuous, even incompetent; a child in an adult world. And so, with just two weeks before leaving my family in Los Angeles and heading off to my first great adult adventure, I set it as a personal challenge to take that rite of passage, that*

first real step into manhood.
There was no question about it; at some point in the next two
weeks, my bedroom had to be thoroughly cleaned.

It got a very big laugh, I have to say. No stranger to comedy (I'd tried stand-up for a summer when I was sixteen), it felt good to know I could take such ready control of a room full of people, with just a bit of clever misdirection.

I didn't return to writing for some time; but when I did, I went at it full-bore. Music was my first love, but writing became the love of my life. I read every book on the subject, finding I could extricate at least one valu- able thing from each book. I started writing novels, knowing I had mountains to climb before I had the necessary skills. But I'd had the same experience before, learning through painful hours of study and practice, in music. That prepared me to put myself through the long, lonely years required to master fiction.

I fell in love with the puzzle that was good writing. Structure, emotion, detail, tension and release; the same principles could be applied to fiction as to song-writ- ing, and I was ready to learn one, as I had learned the other.

I also found the same release I had found in music, the same way to express myself and use the best of my talents to truly connect to other people. Unlike with my music, I didn't need to rely on other musicians or drag my family out to nightclubs. I could work alone, and I could make the final decisions. Writing a novel is like making a movie, it's been said, wherein the author is the writer, di- rector, producer, set designer, and heads of the lighting and costume and props departments. They also play every role.

And whereas songs were limited to three minutes and one clever concept (they often lack even these), novels gave me the kind of canvas I wanted; much broad- er and deeper, to allow me to plumb the delicacies of human behavior.

It was around this time that Kindle gave new life to the publishing industry. Suddenly, my skills were in demand. It was a slow climb from there. I always lent the greatest artistry I could, even to some of the post- Fifty Shades short stories I was hired to write. I worked for peanuts, but came up the ranks, until I was earning at the top level of my field. I've had dozens of clients, whose glowing reviews and five-star ratings have helped me earn a reputation for excellence, one which has given me a career. Over the course of that career, I've written screenplays and stage plays, nonfiction, and fiction, in just about every genre. Over hundreds of books and story series, I've learned what works, what doesn't, and why.

Part of writing is looking for help, having people read and critique your work. Another part of writing is teaching; reading and critiquing the work of others. I have found both to be excellent ways to learn. But as I developed, I sought guidance less and less and began to offer it more and more. In classes, workshops, and even casual conversation, I loved talking about the elements of fiction (and I still do); the three-act structure, the structure of a scene and a sequel (no, not the second movie in a series), the necessity of a good subplot, the types of heroes. I've developed techniques which earn me universal praise, and which are simple and effective. I know how to create the fictive bubble, that trance-like state which makes the reader feel as if the action were happening all around them, as if they were in the book themselves.

I also know how to break that bubble. I've made every mistake in the book(s), I'm happy to say. Because I learned more from my mistakes, and I can (and do) help others to avoid those mistakes, to sidestep them and use time-tested techniques to avoid common traps, which stymie good writers and good stories alike. I know every building block of good writing, from the macro to the micro, and I'm more than happy to share them with anybody who is eager to learn. I think that might be you.

I hope so.

And it hardly matters who you are. Whether you are a beginner or an advanced writer, there's always some- thing new to learn. Believe me, if there is something about writing fiction that I don't know, I want to know it. Chances are, you possess that same strong drive to master the mechanics and the philosophy behind one of the great art forms in all of human experience (and, along with cave paintings, one of the first).

I will guide you through the entire writing process, from choosing a genre to the principles of story and character; through details of outlining, technique, structure, editing, and more. I'll present some of my best writing prompts and exercises to help you master the elements of fiction, including action, suspense, humor, and romance. This book is meant to be read and reread, to be used as a reference, a workbook, a checklist to help you keep track of the myriad elements that good fiction juggles on every page, in every sentence, with every word.

Great writing strengthens the mind and the character of both the writer and the reader. It cultivates empathy and a continuous quest to learn more. It is the very expression of the soul. It is the essence of self-actualiza- tion, because only the individual can become a writer; they're made, not born, and they're self-made too.

Writing can bring more than personal satisfaction and a good paycheck (or a lot more than that). Writing can bring glory and cultural immortality, but these are not the right reasons to take it up. There are easier ways to fail to become famous, believe me. But if you want to join the ranks of Ernest Hemingway, Stephen King, J.K. Rowling, or even William Shakespeare; if you want to touch others the way these writers did and continue to do and will go on doing; if you want to achieve true mastery of fiction, then you're already on the right track. The first step was reading this introduction; the next step is to read the rest of book.

You'll have to do the work, but you won't be alone. You've got a roadmap through this strange place, a guide to see you through. Welcome to the myste- rious world of fiction; where fantasy and reality collide, where past and pres- ent meet, where lies and the truth become one, where life and love are always pushed to the limit, and where you are the master of it all.

And, in case you're wondering, the story about my bedroom was true and, ulti- mately, I just had my partner do it for me. Now, let's get to work!

1

THE SECRET TO WRITING IS … WRITING

"Start writing, no matter what. The water does not flow until the faucet is turned on."

— BY LOUIS L'AMOUR

I once interviewed SCTV head writer, Dave Thomas, about his memoir. He told me he found the hardest part of being a writer was to actually sit down and do the writing. On the other hand, he considered every written page like money in the bank; once it was there, it could be lost or stolen or nurtured and used to contribute to a greater sum, but at least it was there.

Because, for a lot of writers, the real challenge is just to sit down and do it. And this is down to a lot of things. No matter who you are or where you are in your writer's journey, you're likely to have to deal with some of these things. Every writer hits a block somewhere along the line, and many more start there. And, as in all things, you must know what you're dealing with, in order to deal with it effectively.

Writer's Block

If you're reading this book, it's probably because you're having a hard time pushing your writing forward. It could be that you've been trying and failed, or that what's worked for you before isn't working so well anymore. Maybe only now, you're coming to realize that what you've been doing hasn't worked so well and it's time for a new approach.

Or it could be that you're blocked. This happens, and can strike at any time in the writing process. It may be at the beginning, with the dreaded and intimidating blank page. It may be midway through the story, in the long and complex Act Two.

Leo Tolstoy (War and Peace) and Virginia Woolf (Mrs. Dalloway) both suffered from writer's block at different times in their careers, and each overcame it. Harry Potter's J.K. Rowling battled with it, as the result of a lawsuit. Toni Morrison (Beloved) used rituals before writing, to prepare/program herself into a readiness to write. Jack London (Call of the Wild) used daily word- count goals to prevent writer's block and write his many famous books. Fantasy writer Neil Gaiman (The Sandman) suggests getting away from the writing for a while, to refresh one's perspective and clear the mind.

But let's presume you're not quite so far along in your career. The most common causes of writer's block early in a project or career are a lack of time and a lack of confidence.

Time and Confidence

Writing requires a great deal of two things primarily; time and confidence. It takes an incredible amount of both of these precious and fleeting qualities to become a writer. However, given ample amounts of both, there's no reason anybody of reasonable intelligence shouldn't be able to write well and to finish what they start.

Time is crucial to experience. And I don't mean time reading books, or reading about writing. There is no substitute for actually doing it. That is where the lessons and theories and concepts become real. I wrote my first four novels concurrently, over two years. I knew I was making mistakes, and new mistakes with each book, but I learned from them. I could then take those lessons to the other books, to apply the lessons I'd learned. At that time in my life, however, I was fortu- nate enough to have time to write. An insurance settle- ment meant I didn't need a full-time job. So I could devote all my time to writing, to reading about writing, to immersing myself in the craft of writing.

The bottom line is, that any person who wishes to write must do it, and to do it, one must find the time. But most people have full-time jobs, sometimes two jobs plus children to raise. There are precious memories to be savored, bills to be paid, intimate relationships that need to be nurtured. In today's frantical-ly-paced soci- ety, time is of even greater value than ever before. The easiest thing to set aside for more pressing concerns is writing. And there's nothing unreasonable about this.

Given the choice of spending time with one's child or sitting alone with a lap-top writing something nobody may ever read, it's easy to choose time with your child. That's a choice to be proud of.

But if you want to be a writer, you must find time; time to read and time to write. A lot of people will tell you that, until you've written one million words (1,000,000), you have no business calling yourself a writer. Others will tell you that you're not likely to make a dime at anything, until you've put in at least ten thousand hours (10,000). That's over two hours a day, every day of the year, including holidays and workdays, for ten years, to clock your ten thousand hours.

Luckily, you have this book, which will make the old adage seem like just that. In essence, I've done your ten thousand hours for you (and your million words plus, every year, for over a decade). But you'll still need time to dedicate to your writing.

The best way to do this is to schedule writing time into your life and to stick to that schedule. Don't worry too much about the million words. It's about making the time to sit down and write, no matter how much you actually produce. So, think about how you can work a regular writing shift into your daily life.

Here are things to consider when you do:

Writing is hard to do sporadically. It takes momentum, and it takes confidence. But it's hard to work up confi- dence (and even harder to work up momentum) in brief periods, separated by great spans of time. A one-hour writing session may sound good, but you may also just be warming up by the close of that hour. Your next hour-long session may also be hobbled by warmup time. Try to schedule two hours or more, if you can.

Writing is harder to do at night. It requires a brain that is fresh and filled with protein. After a day of office work and family life, the brain has exhausted much of its nutrient supply. But that's just the physiological aspect of the brain. The mind is also tired, cluttered with events of the day, concerns that will be distracting to a writer. So, reconsider scheduling nightly writing sessions, unless your weekends don't allow for it.

Weekends are best, though we all know that as many people work on the weekends as they do the weekdays. Some people work eight days out of every ten, instead of the traditional five days to every seven.

But your days away from work are the days you should earmark for your writing sessions. It will be hard if you have familial obligations, of course. But it can be done!

Since the brain is freshest in the morning, uncluttered, and since a sizeable timespan is needed to advance a writer on his or her journey, consider scheduling your writing sessions for early in the morning on the week- ends. Ernest Hemingway only wrote in the mornings! You may not be a so-called morning person, but the physiological fact is that you could be, if you changed your schedule. Take a few weeks to alter your sleeping habits, and you can become a morning person. Wake up early, shower, pour a cup of coffee and get to work. Give yourself two hours, while your partner sees to the kids (if you have any or all of these). Two hours won't be much, but it's a good place to start. Do that for two days consecutively and you've got four hours clocked for the week.

Keep it regular. Remember that your brain will lose track of your momentum, of the details of the story, motifs and other things you may be developing. So try not to let too much time go by between sessions. One week is the longest you should go without writing.

And don't skip a week. It's not that the whole project will implode, but it becomes all the more likely that you will skip another week. When (and if) you get back to the project, you'll be so disconnected by time that your confidence may be shaken. This is a huge trigger for writer's block.

Start off slow. If you've got more than two hours at a stretch, go for it. But writing is both physically and mentally draining. It can be hard on the eyes, on the hands, on the back, and on the brain. So don't commit yourself to eight hours at a shot, straight off the bat. If you're new, limit yourself to at most a five-hour session at first. If you want to keep going, go ahead. But you may be setting yourself up for feeling like a failure, if you commit to a schedule that is too demanding. This will rob you of your confidence. But you'll likely find that you want more time to write, and you'll start working on the weekdays.

Take a note here that these are writing sessions. You can and should be spending other time reading about writing, as you're doing now. Your writing sessions will be where you put what you learn here and in other books to use. We are going to be including exercises, of course, so you can put these lessons to immediate use. But your novel or other piece of longform fiction will require further and frequent reuse of the techniques you'll learn here. It's also worthy of note that we will be focusing on novels here, and spending several chapters on the techniques of the written word, over that of the spoken or performed word. Many of the concepts, such as the importance of time and confidence to any writer, apply to any media, across the board. This is actually true of any art form, from dancing to architecture, as well as any sport or other physical skill.

If you've got the confidence, go for it. The more confi- dence you have, the more you'll be moved to write and to learn. The less confidence you have, the more apt you will be to fall back on excuses and give up the book before finishing it.

Common Excuses

Confidence is so crucial, because time alone will not see any writer through. There is so much time required, confidence is likely to wane without meas- urable results. A sense of futility may sink in; this is what sabotages countless writers and their writing careers. A sense of pointlessness is what results in unfinished tales, and that is often due to time spent without results to foster confidence. You'll know it when you hear it, especially in your own voice:

- *"I'm just not a writer."*
- *"The story didn't make sense."*
- *"It was a dumb idea anyway."*
- *"Why bother? Nobody's ever going to read it anyway."*
- *"There just wasn't enough time."*

But these are excuses, and none of them hold up to even the slightest scrutiny. As I've said, anybody with the time and confidence and intelligence to obtain a working understanding of the principles of writing can become a writer. True, some people will be more natu- rally drawn to it, or their natural gifts may make it easier for them. But it's not like being a pro ball player or dancer. No amount of time or confidence will give you gifts such as the natural, requisite grace of a dancer or a great athlete. A writer can write, no matter their body shape or physical skill. If you're not a writer, it's because you didn't make the time to become one.

If the story didn't make sense, it's because the writer didn't understand the mechanics of writing, including story and scene structure, character, dialogue, and other things you'll learn here. If the story was a dumb idea, perhaps it was simply underdeveloped. The writer didn't take the time or effort to redream the dream and let the story find its own form. The great film Dr. Strangelove... began life as a drama and became a dark comedy only during preproduction. And that was only because the comparable drama, Fail Safe, was already in production. Dean Martin's successful Matt Helm film series became a comedy during production, because the first installment was a laughably bad action film.

The defeatist notion that nobody will read a given book anyway is hard to support. The internet has made it more possible than ever to find an audience. In previous generations, Random House and Penguin and the other big gatekeeper publishers kept independent authors out of the public eye. But that is no longer the case. At no time in history has an unknown writer had so much access to such a broad reading audience.

In any case, not everybody writes to reach a huge audi- ence. And even those who do have to realize that you write for yourself first. Since nobody else may ever read the book, it should certainly please the writer first.

So, it just comes down to time. Well, I'm here to help you make the most of your efforts, to cut down your learning curve, as much as I can. Take my ten thousand hours; may they serve you well. But they won't do much for you without your own determination and confidence and, of course, your precious time. However much time I can save you, you'll still have to invest some of your own.

Remain confident that your sacrifice of time is neither pointless nor futile.

Use a Timeline

Think ahead. Once you've committed to writing, commit to a timeline. Estimate your book to be 40,000 words and pick a completion date. Imagine you make this your New Year's resolution. You might timeline it this way:

- 40,000 words per year

- 10,000 words per quarter

- 2,500 words per month

- 625 words per week

- 312.5 words per session (2 sessions per week)

- 156.25 words per hour

To give you an idea, an average page on Windows Word or Pages (for Mac) is about 300 words per page. So if you stick to this timeline, you'll have your rough draft in one year, with just a half-page written per hour. Can you double that? If you can, just write one full page per hour, and you'll have your first draft done in six months. Then you can do a timeline for finishing the book with rewrites and the like.

Use your timeline to track your progress and make sure you don't fall behind.

The Pomodoro Method

Writing is the essence of this famous office management method. The idea is that a big project with a longer timeline is broken down into smaller projects with shorter timelines. The completion of each smaller task (called Pomodoros) brings confidence and a sense of accomplishment, which are short-term rewards on the way to the bigger rewards of career advancement and success, which come from the completion of the long- term goal. That confidence helps the completion of further milestones. This method also ensures that the project follows a timeline (each Pomodoro has a dead- line, as does the long-term goal). If the Pomodoros are completed on time, the long-term goal should be completed on time.

Books, whether fiction or nonfiction, are themselves comprised of a series of chapters, smaller units leading to the completion of the long-term project, which is the book itself. Each chapter should contribute to a sense of being informed, of being increasingly capable, of greater confidence. Think of your outline as a Pomodoro, each chapter as another one, the first draft a bigger one; all are achievable goals, which help the writer progress on the journey toward a completed book.

A Time ... and a Place

Taking time is crucial, but it's also important to set aside the proper place to write. A good writing area should be:

- Readily available
- Private
- Quiet
- Free of distractions
- Comfortable
- Well-lit
- Well-ventilated
- Uncluttered

Remember that a lot of people don't have an extra room that can be turned into a study. But any room can become a study, with a good lamp, a desk, a chair, and a door to close. A guest bedroom would work perfectly, or even a corner of your master bedroom may be perfectly adequate.

Make sure to get a decent chair. Hours in a bad chair can wreak all kinds of havoc on your back and shoul- ders, your arms and hands. Armrests are strongly recommended.

Tips and Tricks

Once you're writing, the idea is to keep writing. You've got the time and the place. You'll have your working outline, so you won't be stuck for what to write next. Even so, writing sometimes requires a little push to get started or keep it going. Some writers use word sprints. Like micro-Pomodoros, a writer shoots for a thousand words, or as many as they can write in a given time. Along these lines, writers will generally assign them- selves goals for any particular writing session, such as the end of the scene, end of the chapter, end of the act. It depends on where the writer is in the story.

Make other, longer-term goals, which you share with others. This gives you accountability and will add just enough pressure to help you meet your goals, without being so crushing that it derails the motivation.

You may think about keeping a writer's journal; things you did right, mistakes you have the opportunity to learn from, things which got in the way of your productivity and can be avoided (and how to avoid them).

Make writing an everyday practice. You won't neces- sarily want to schedule a daily multi-hour session, but even beyond reading about writing between sessions, you should still write something every day. Write a letter, make some notes about your book, keep a journal of things to use for inspiration (turns of phrase, personality quirks). To help with this, we'll turn to our first session of writing prompts.

Prompts

These prompts will get you through any of the things we're going to be looking at in this book. They are great just to get the ideas and the writing energy flowing. Sometimes, a little push is all it takes, and that's what these prompts are all about.

Write a letter to your lead character. Make mention of a few things which may come up in the story. Ask the character some questions, address them like an old friend or a professional associate. This will establish the character as real in your imagination, a person whose story needs to be told. Writing about the details just a little bit may even generate new story ideas.

Write a letter as your lead character to you, the writer. This will give a voice to your character, and his or her concerns are bound to rise to the fore. Let your char- acter be instructive to the writer, even demanding. This will give you the feeling of accountability.

Post both letters on the wall over your desk, for a quick-glance reminder from time to time, as a continuous prompt.

Exercises

To give you a leg up on time management, put together your writing schedule. Work it out. If you have trouble finding time, prioritize your activities and think of one or two you can eliminate or perhaps reduce. Be realistic and start with a schedule you know you can maintain. You can always increase it as you go, and you probably will. Too much time allocated to writing at the start can be dangerous, too.

To give yourself a leg up on confidence, try this exer- cise: Pick any three nouns out of the dictionary, making sure they're chosen at random. Set a timer for five minutes. You must pick one of the three words to appear in your first sentence. Use the other two some- where in the first paragraph.

Keep writing for the rest of the five minutes. Don't overthink it, don't edit it, don't ponder the possibilities. Just keep writing, as if from instinct alone. Then read it back. You'll probably find the results are better than you expected! That should give you confidence enough to sit down and start writing your book.

But before you do that, stay seated and keep reading!

2

THINK LIKE A MAGPIE: IDEA
GENERATION AND COLLECTION

Now that the *when* and the *where* of your writing is resolved, the next question becomes the *what*.

If you're writing fiction, you need a story to write, a premise to realize. You need a plot and characters, and then dialogue and prose. And for all this, you have to have an idea.

Everything starts with the idea, the notion, the flicker of inspiration. But this can be mysterious, ethereal. One cannot control or even generate inspiration, try though one might (by whatever means available). Plato said that artists are like prisms to catch and diffract the light of inspiration. But it's not enough to stand around and wait for inspiration to strike. The writer has to harvest these ideas, and know how to write, even when inspira- tion fails. Inspired or not, I could come up with five writable plots in half as many minutes.

First of all, ideas come from a variety of sources. There's no single right way to do it. Like a lot of things, these methods vary, from writer to writer. Different people have different techniques, which work for them. But all artists have to understand what techniques are apt to generate which results, if only to have a broader mastery of their craft. More often than not, new tech- niques may solve old and ongoing problems.

And for finding ideas, the techniques are as varied as in anything else.

A lot of famous authors have unique ways of finding inspiration for their sto- ries. Stephen King (*Carrie*) seems to foster an imaginary friend, who appears to him with one-line plotlines, and that seems entirely fitting. Neil Gaiman writes his notions down in note- books, as did Roald Dahl (*Charlie and the Chocolate Factory*).

J.R.R. Tolkien (*The Hobbit*) wrote down a single sentence to inspire his volumes of work.

Peter Benchley and William Peter Blatty were both inspired by news report- age of true-life events to write their greatest books (*JAWS and The Exorcist*, respective- ly). Truman Capote's In Cold Blood and Hunter S. Thompson's *Hell's Angels*, among his other books, began life as reportage and evolved into greater works in their own right.

Charles Bukowski found inspiration in his own life, documenting it in a long and profitable series of books, covering different epochs of his life. His al- ter-ego, Hank Chinaski, is always the central character.

If you're having trouble with finding something to write, try some of these techniques.

Draw from your life. When they say, "Write what you know," this is what they mean.

First, a note: In general, I go by a modified rule, as this one is a bit constrictive. Remember that William Peter Blatty never exorcised a demon from a child; he didn't even investigate the case. Mario Puzo (*The Godfather*) wasn't in the mafia. They didn't restrict themselves to what they knew from their own direct experience. They did the research necessary to make those worlds come alive as they did. Rather, they wrote what they knew *to be true*. Fiction is about fact in this way; it is the truth of the characters and their actions that makes good fiction. The universal truths of courage or cowardice, of risk and reward, of individual and family, faith or knowledge, of integrity or duplicity, honor and dishonor; the very truths of the human experience are reflected in fiction. We'll take a closer look at these themes later in the book. So take the phrase *Write what you know* with a grain of salt, at least for now.

The original saying is relevant to us here. There is inspiration in every household. Every good character is complex, and every human being is complex (even those who may seem the simplest). So, look to the people you know, the stories of their lives. Perhaps they have qualities of character which, if put into an entirely different setting, would make an exceptional story (called *a fish out of water* story). The countless deriva- tions of Mark Twain's A *Connecticut Yankee* in King Author's Court are all fish out of water stories. A man who is fairly ordinary in his own time becomes extraordinary in a different era. Eddie Murphy's film comedy *Coming to America* is such a story as well, though the cultural shift is not time-oriented, but distance-oriented.

Or your family's lives may have plenty of inspiration, just as they are. Remember that inspiration is not an idea, and an idea is not a story. Each is the spark which ignites the next, one step which introduces the one after. Inspiration gives you an idea, then story gives life and voice to that inspiration. That's what this book is essentially about.

My family, for example, endured a tragedy in which my beloved father, his second wife, their daughter and his mother-in-law, all perished. That was the inspiration. The idea was this: What if his wife had survived, and how would her relationships with the surviving step- sons evolve? I wound up using only two surviving stepchildren and made them both girls. That was the idea. The story, told alternatingly in the present and in the past, fleshed out that idea.

A lot of stories are generated by the phrase *What if?* Almost any transformation story uses this basis, for example Franz Kafka's *The Metamorphosis*. It asks the question, *What if a man woke up one morning to find that he'd been transformed into a giant cockroach?* This fanciful notion is popular in modern screen comedies like Big (*what if a little boy woke up to find that he'd been trans-formed into an adult*) and the oft-remade *Freaky Friday* (*what if a parent and child switched bodies*).

But this goes beyond transformation stories. *JAWS, The Exorcist, The Terminator, The Abyss* all have *what if* premises. Novels of this sort include Richard Dreyfuss' *The Two Georges*, set in a present in which the Revolutionary War had been lost and North America remained under pseudo-British rule. Mary Shelley's *Frankenstein* has a *what if* premise, and so does Herman Melville's *Moby Dick*.

It's what Hollywood calls *high concept*; stories that aren't apt to happen in real life, but which would happen in the real world under otherwise real-world cir-cum- stances.

We'll take a more in-depth look at setting later in this book, but this can cer-tainly be a powerful way to generate story ideas. Setting is crucial to *fish out of water* stories, clearly (the setting is the water). But the setting can be its own lead character, like Tolkien's Middle Earth, or the backwater Columbian towns of the work of Gabriel Garcia-Marquez. In the modern publishing world, a central aspect of any romantic thriller continues to be an exotic location. Every James Bond novel (and film) features one, as do most run-of-the-mill romance books. Every exotic city represents a new culture, and those cultures will have political conflicts and challenges to propel virtually any story.

Other good ways of generating and harvesting ideas include keeping a writ-er's journal. Use it to note down names, notions, themes, dialogue, character quirks, psychological concepts, historical dates, anything you may use later.

Get out more. You'll find more inspiration and more ideas if you're exposed to more things; new things, new people, new places. Museums are excellent places to generate ideas; a painting can lead to a story, or an installation. I personally saw an art piece about the destroyed abolitionist gathering place, Philadelphia Hall, which inspired a novel based on the events.

Look to other stories. I'm not suggesting that you steal a story outright, of course. But it's also true that there are a limited number of basic stories. If you know your stories well, you'll know what kind of story you're telling, and that will help you tell it. Experts differ on how many root stories there are. Some say twenty, some say seven, some say two, some say only one. And virtually every story is a twist on one of these basic plots. I'll offer some examples, but here's the shorthand:

First, virtually any story is told in the three-act struc- ture, which we will go into in greater detail later. But this structure is often used in the very popular story paradigm called *The Hero's Journey*. Best presented by Joseph Campbell's seminal work, *Hero of a Thousand Faces*, the hero's journey may be called the only real plot. This is because so many other stories use the hero's journey, which is always in three acts, that the two have become synonymous. The film version of *The Wizard of Oz* is often cited as a classic example of both the hero's journey and the three-act structure. Even the fact-based novel *Papillon* perfectly fits both overlapping structures. The Harry Potter books all favor both the hero's journey and the three-act structure. Furthermore, even stories that are not hero's journey stories still generally use the three-act structure.

So, a lot of people will tell you there's only one story, and that's the hero's journey. If you want to write a story, just write that. You may or may not agree. But in terms of writing your own book, the three-act struc- ture is just a little bit ahead of where we are now. The hero's journey is something you should know now, though we'll also look at it in greater detail later.

If there is not one story but two, which besides the hero's journey is the second story? Well, the answer to this question doesn't include the hero's journey (it more or less assumes it). If there are only two stories, they are likely to be identified as either *Cinderella* or *Romeo and Juliet*, both of which are three-act struc- tures and hero's journey stories as well, in their own way. Every romance is essentially one or the other. It comes down to the conflict, which we'll look at in greater detail soon. If there's a fish-out-of-water element to romantic conflict, if there is any kind of transformation at the heart of the story, it's likely in the *Cinderella* tradition. If the conflict is familial and not class-oriented, lacking in transformations or fantastic elements, it is likely in the *Romeo and Juliet* tradition.

But this doesn't include a variety of other classic stories, such as those of betray- al, or of physical quest. But both are found in either fairy tales or the works of William Shakespeare. Any story of a lost child, from *Pinocchio* to the Original Oz books (notably hero's journey stories), echoes *Little Red Riding Hood* or *Hansel and Gretel*. Stories of greed and lust trace back tradi- tionally to Shakespeare's *Othello*. Stories of family duplicity and betrayal find their inspiration in *Macbeth*, *Hamlet*, and *King Lear*.

So, if you're lost for inspiration, take a look at fairy tales or Shakespeare. Hey, everybody else does it.

Emotions can generate entire pieces. Erich Segal's popular *Love Story* is such a book, offering little more than sentiment (but a ton of it, admittedly). Marsha Norman's *'Night, Mother*, plays entirely on the emotions of sorrow and frustration.

You could also try the internet. Online plot and first- line generators, keyword generators, and online forums are all available to authors, anywhere in the world, at no cost.

Prompts

If you can't think of any story ideas, try a prompt. Start with the genre you want to write in and design a story that would be appropriate for that. A spy thriller like *The Hunt for Red October* will lean heavily on the three- act hero's journey tropes. A tearjerker like *The Bridges of Madison County* will have less plot but will turn on sentiment and emotion. If you're writing an emotional story, list a few emotions to find one you think you could generate with a certain story; political zeal, personal responsibility, whatever.

Exercises

If you're really stuck for ideas or want something completely new, try this: Take any book and randomly pick five words. Make sure they're not too short or boring (no pronouns or conjunctions) but mix nouns and verbs and even adjectives, if you can. I just picked these five:

- Against
- Evening
- Visit
- Creative
- Directions

The exercise is to write as many story ideas as you can using those five words:

- An evening visit gives a young creative new direction.
- Creative directions turn against two young people one stormy evening.
- A new law's directions against creative people pits brother against brother.

And so on. Try a few yourself with new words!

Here's another exercise: Google a few smash words and see what headlines come up. Use words like *buried, disappeared, married, chased,* whatever words fit your genre or simply amuse you. You'll be surprised at what comes up and it may just inspire a news-oriented story, like *JAWS.*

A word map is a good exercise. Write an event or notion in the center of a piece of paper. It could be something like WWII, a wedding, a snow storm, a buried treasure, a comet heading toward Earth, restored dinosaurs, a ten-year-old chess genius; it hardly matters. Draw a circle around it. Then draw a line out from the center circle to reach another circle above or to the side of the original. Fill the empty circle with something which would be related or affected in some way: A young pilot in WWII, a scientist in the restored dinosaurs event, the parents of the genius. Then do another, jutting out from the same inner circle. These are the elements of the story you could write, the subplots and supporting characters.

Whatever method you use, you've now come to under- stand in greater detail how an idea can be found and nurtured. The next question is *How?* The answer to that lies with one of the most mysterious, mercurial, and controversial aspects of fiction.

The outline.

3

MAKING YOUR ROADMAP

Outlines mean different things to different people. And every different writer has his or her own idea of what an outline is or should be. The idea isn't to enforce one idea or the other, but to cast a new light on this controversial part of the writing process.

Here we have a spectrum of gradients, with one extreme being a writer who plots rigorously (called *plotters* by some) and the other extreme being a writer who plots not at all (lately called a *pantser*, as they write by the seat of their pants).

JK Rowling plotted her Harry Potter books rigorously, and John Grisham did the same with his popular legal thrillers, rarely if ever varying from their outlines.

Stephen King seems to favor story over plot and eschews outlining as restrictive. George R.R. Martin (*Game of Thrones*) seems to deprioritize plotting, as well.

But the majority of writers fall somewhere in between, and that probably includes you. You may not be sure about how outlining will serve you best, or you may be frustrated with your current outlining techniques and are looking for a new approach.

Drawbacks and Benefits of Both Approaches

Rigorous plotters always know what's coming up next. They aren't subject to those sleepless nights or long walks or bouts of writer's block. They have a good idea of where they'll wind up, so they're risking less. Their work is more tightly regimented, so they're more likely to stick to timelines.

But rigorously plotted stories may be predictable. They rarely take on unique structures, characters become stock and perform their story functions in an oft- perfunctory manner.

The time dedicated to writing an outline is likely to be less than the amount of time dedicated to writing. Months may go by for an outline (and that feels like a lot) but years can be spanned during the writing of a book (not at all uncommon). So, a year or two after making your first group of choices, you are not allowing yourself to be affected by that time in your life, by things you've learned. You're presupposing that you've learned nothing you can put into the book, that you're no better a story writer than you were when you started.

This writer also denies themselves the opportunity to surprise themselves, and thereby create new devices and techniques they can use in later books, adding to their overall style.

The so-called *pantser* has plenty of room to be inspired and flexible, that's true. But this is also the writer who often gets stuck, particularly at the very beginning or in the long and unruly act two. The pantser may lose track of the plot, of what has already happened or what they just intended to write, but perhaps never did. The panster may lose track of the proper proportions of the overall three-act structure, resulting in some being way too long and others being way too short. The pantser may have no ending in mind, and therefore may find themselves meandering, stuck with a story that doesn't have a satisfying ending. True, he may not know who did it, but the pantser may not even be sure how to get everybody into the same room for the big reveal.

The Beat Sheet and the Road Map

The first thing to do is give up the idea of an outline as just one thing. Because a story is never just one thing. Everything that happens, every scene (where action happens) and sequel (where inaction happens) has two levels; what is happening and how it is happening. The *what* is from the author's perspective; this is what has to happen, in order for the story to move along. Often called a beat sheet, it may look like this:

- Act 1
- Inciting incident
- Intro hero
- Intro heroine
- Conflict between hero and heroine
- Call to action
- Refusal of the call
- Plot point 1

And so on. These are the things which have to happen. We have to meet the hero, he has to meet the heroine. There doesn't have to be a refusal of the call, but there must be a call to action. This is a bullet-point list of the 'what' aspects of a story.

The *how* refers to the more detailed physical aspects of the events. If this is a murder mystery, the inciting inci- dent will be the murder. Who is the victim? How is the deed accomplished? Keep in mind that these questions will not be answered yet, only raised. Murder scenes that open stories often happen from the victim's point of view, and they often die (murder victims tend to do this). And if it's a mystery, they do not reveal the iden- tity of the killer through their POV during the attack, so that the reader still doesn't know the solution to the mystery.

So the story road map charts how things happen. This may be as detailed as the writer prefers, but it may look something like this:

- Act 1
- Inciting incident: A young swimmer is taken by a great white shark at night, leaving a single witness.
- Intro hero: Police chief, Martin Brody, goes to work and hears the wit- nesses' stories. He begins to investigate.
- Intro villain: The town's mayor wants Brody's investigation shut down for business reasons. The Fourth of July holiday is nearing.

And so on. The *how* of things is made clearer. Some writers will go into great detail here, some allow them- selves to leave the details until they are actually writing the book. Some plot out the hows ahead of time, others only know the basic *whats* of the storyline.

Some road maps will include the goal of the scene, the location of the scene, and other significant details.

The approach I find best is even more of a compromise between the two. I like to know about half of the *what* and little of the *how*. This allows flexibility and the chance for inspiration to suggest new notions, which time and familiarity with the story couldn't afford earlier in the process. But even the *what* should be flexi- ble, in my opinion. This is for several reasons. The first one to recognize is that the *how* can influence the what.

For example, attempting to accomplish a vital task, a character may wind up being injured, and this may be unexpected to the author, as much as to the reader. That's good, as if things are all expected, stories quickly become predictable. It's the unexpected that keeps fiction fresh. But an injured character may change the course of the story, and other goals may come into play. This is especially important in a mystery, where the who (the murderer) may not be known by the author anymore than by the reader. This is the way I prefer to write mysteries. My reasoning is this: If the writer knows who did it, the reader has about a fifty-fifty chance of guessing it correctly, no matter how clever the writer is, no matter how many red herrings are there to misdirect the reader. But if the writer does not know who did it, if the writer discovers it as the story develops (starting with several deliberate possibilities) then the chances of the reader guessing it correctly are drastically reduced. It's still possible, but it's the next best thing to impossible. That takes confidence, however, and knowledge of structure. And if you don't know who, you can't know how. The how will often present the who. The what, however (revealing the murderer), still has to happen.

But mystery or not, stories present opportunities to develop storylines and characters in unexpected ways. Some characters will take on a life of their own, and their increased involvement (from spear carrier to ally or antagonist) may change the course of the story in thrilling and vibrant ways.

It's one of the benefits of being flexible. If you are a rigorous plotter, you're committed to a group of deci- sions you made at one time, early on, before the book had a chance to come to life.

I find it best to have a sketchy beat sheet, largely insuf- ficient by about half, in terms of beats. Because some beats will dictate others, things which happen have to be followed up in ways that will present themselves during the writing, though they may have been over- looked during the conception or outlining. I generally transform my beat sheet into a road map as I go, replacing the *whats* with the *hows*. I'm never lost, because I have my beat sheet, but I'm not restricted by an overly written road map. Yet, looking back, I have a sound record of what I've written and what I can develop. The road map is great as a way of recording the trip; the beat sheet is most efficient for planning the trip.

If you're still stumped, there are various outlining soft- ware packages and services you can look into, including Scrivener, Trello, Scapple, Timeline, Aeon, and Xmind.

The Snowflake Method

This method of outlining is comparable to the word map we examined earlier. It begins with a frank and brief expression of the story's central idea. Characters and subplots do not develop sequentially, in a direct cause-and-effect relationship. Rather, they spring from the same central notion and then interact in a less linear manner. From the central concept, you gradually expand the story outwards, adding more detail with each stage, until you have a complete outline. It has the benefit of not following an empty paradigm; rather, the story may develop organically, creating fresh and surprising events, which are unique to your story.

You're likely to find that, once all is said and done, you're still going to wind up with a solid three-act structure, but this is a different way of getting there. And this book is all about presenting different approaches, more alternatives.

Tips and Tricks

To outline your story to the utmost of its potential, there are other things to keep in mind.

Understand the hallmarks of a great plot. A great plot of almost any genre or structure (which we'll look at shortly) can be broken down this way: A likeable person doing a good deed for others against overwhelming odds. This includes all the hallmarks of plot: A relatable character, high stakes, insurmountable conflict. All good stories have this. Why? Nobody cares about an unlikable character or their personal needs or what they do for themselves. Nor do they care if anybody's needs are serviced without adequate opposition.

Plan subplots: Something happening outside of the main plot but that still affects it, such as a storm or natural force or family feud (if not already in the main plot).

Create character goals: Every character needs to have a goal they feel is admirable and beneficial, though it doesn't necessarily seem that way to others (even villains generally think they're doing the right thing).

Know the function of each scene: Every scene must move the story forward, deepen the characterization, or both. The function is the *what*, not the *how*.

Give equal consideration to all characters and events: Underwritten characters and events only detract from the well-developed material.

Make the outline work for you, rather than the other way around: That's the cardinal rule of outlining!

Prompts

To get your outline mojo flowing, write a quick prequel story for your main character. It doesn't have to relate to the events in the main story, just enough to establish the chain of events a character like this might instigate.

Exercises

Also, make a quick beat sheet of your own book, looking for things that might be missing. Keep it brief.

You may also want to examine each plot point and ask:

- Is this vital? If this scene is removed, what will happen to the rest of the story?

- How does this further the plot or deepen the characterization?

- Is each scene's goal clearly stated or at least implied?
- What plot points are missing?

Take one of your favorite movies and do a beat sheet for it. This will only take as long as it takes to watch the movie. Make it a movie you know, so you're not totally absorbed in it. The key is to write one-line descriptors of every scene.

Then watch the movie again, this time describing every scene in greater detail, as you might do in a more fully realized road map.

Now that you're clear on how you want to go about outlining your idea, it's time to take a closer look at what you'll be outlining. It's the highway that takes you from the beginning of your story to its end; it's what happens.

The plot.

4

STORY STRUCTURE MATTERS: HOW TO CREATE A KILLER PLOT

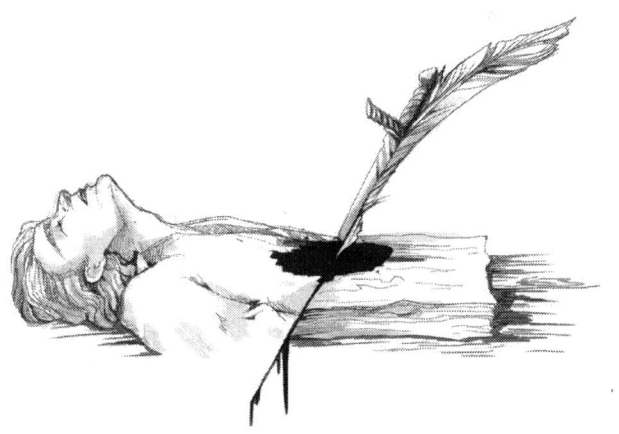

Now that we've looked at how to outline, it's time to look at what we're outlining, and that's plot.

There are a variety of sound story structures, and they each have their own particularities.

The first thing any writer or would-be writer should do is to read. Read as many novels as you can of the genre you wish to write in. Read the best books you can find in other genres, too.

But don't just read them like a reader. You have to learn to read like a writer.

Read Like a Writer

A reader can allow him- or herself to let the story wash over them, to entrance them; and that's just what well- written fiction does. It's known as the *fictive dream* or the *fictive bubble*, and we'll talk more about that soon. As a writer, you have to understand how it works, to analyze it, and to resist it. You have to read with a more critical and analytical eye. It's a different way of read- ing, and you can only develop it through deliberate practice and experience. And if the book is well writ- ten, it's even harder. A good writer can entrance even the most stubbornly resistant reader.

Consider reading a few good books twice. Yes, it's a greater time commitment. But you'll be able to read it through once, as a reader, letting the story wash over you, without constant questioning and correcting (this is reading like an editor). Then, the second time, read it with an analytical eye, with the intention of decoding what the author is presenting. This book will give you the keys to that intricate code, piece by piece.

The basic piece concerning us here is plot. So read something short and snappy, like *Portnoy's Complaint* (Phillip Roth) or the short novel *Harold & Maude* (Colin Higgins), or Ken Kesey's masterpiece *One Flew Over the Cuckoo's Nest.* I person- ally cannot recommend Catcher in the Rye, though it is short enough for this exercise. John Steinbeck has a few good short novels which will work, such as *The Pearl or The Grapes of Wrath.* F. Scott Fitzgerald's seminal *The Great Gatsby* will work too. All these books are quick reads, with varyingly well-struc- tured plots. Read them once as a reader, then read them a second time as a writer. Make notes. Create outlines of the books, reverse-engineering them to better understand how and why they work.

An Example: A Game of Thrones

Here's a breakdown of the plot of the first A Game of Thrones book, to better help you understand how story structure looks and functions.

Chapters 1-6 (8.3% into the story):

DRAMATIC PHASE ONE: The Setup

Principal characters and the story world are introduced, ongoing subplots are established and the foundations for the central conflict (the main plot) are established.

ACT ONE: The Imperfect Situation

Ned Stark (a common character) is presented with various conflicts (the imperfect situation) caused or exploited by the king (an oppressive antagonist). Each wants to lead Winterfell for good or for ill (a conflicting goal). The death of the King's Hand, Arryn (a disturbance) instigates a request by the king to relocate Ned to the capi- tal, to occupy the vacated position (a dilemma), which means the common character must shapeshift into a new role (Hand of the King) to achieve the initial goal.

Chapters 7-20 (19.4% into the story):

ACT TWO: Learning the Rules of an Unfamiliar Situation

Ned learns the complexities of navigating the King's court (unfamiliar situation) and faces the manipulation of people around the king (inci- dental opposition), as he travels to King's Landing to serve as the Hand of the King and investigate the mysterious circumstances of his friend's death (transitional goal). A renewed family feud between the houses of Stark and Lannister creates an assassination attempt (a reality check), securing Ned's resolve to prove that the Lannister family killed the previous King's Hand (the commitment).

DRAMATIC PHASE TWO: Confrontation

Chapters 21-45 (34.7% into the story)

ACT THREE: Stumbling into the Central Conflict

Ned clashes with the Lannister clan (central conflict), as he faces opposition from the King and his court (intentional opposition). Ned tries to expose them (false goal). A kidnapping prompts revenge against Ned (a turn) and Ned learns the reason for the first Hand's killing. Ned uses the solution to compel an antagonist to leave the king's court (in a moment of truth).

ACT FOUR: Implementing a Doomed Plan

Chapters 46- 58 (62.4% into the story)

Ned implements a doomed plan against the counsel of his advisors (self-inflicted opposition) and installs the King's brother as king (penulti- mate goal). Ned is betrayed and taken prisoner (a low point), but he can save his daughter by confessing treason (a newfound resolve for the ultimate goal).

DRAMATIC PHASE THREE: Resolution

ACT FIVE: Taking a Long Shot

Chapters 59-65 (80.5% into the story)

Ned confesses (a long shot) and is ridiculed (ulti- mate opposition) before being beheaded (all is lost).

ACT SIX: Living in a New Situation

Chapters 65-72 (90.2% into the story)

Having accomplished (or failed to have accom- plished) the ultimate goal, the character is shown living in a New Situation.

Ned's execution causes an uproar (the new situa- tion), creating a chain of events to be followed up in following *Game of Thrones* installments.

As I said, that's a breakdown of A Game of Thrones. I hope it has been helpful in breaking down a long, complex story (essentially a hero's journey and a three- act structure at its core) into understandable pieces.

Let's take a closer look at the more conventional struc- tures. You may be surprised at what you find!

The Three-Act Structure & The Hero's Journey

While not precisely the same, these two are so closely related that they bear examination side-by-side. The three-act structure has been used for hundreds of years. Even the five-act play structure used by Shakespeare, Voltaire, Moliere, and before them all the way back to the playwrights of Ancient Greece, created stories that fit the three-act structure. The seven-act structure, which we'll discuss shortly, likewise correlates to the three-act structure. So does A Game of Thrones, but we'll get to that.

The three-act structure works basically like this:

Act 1

- Inciting Incident
- Refusal of the call to action
- Further complication (plot point 1)

Act 2

- Acceptance of the call
- Border guard incident 1
- Border guard incident 2
- Reversal of fortune (midpoint)
- Rising conflict 1

- Rising conflict 2
- Low point (Plot Point 2)

Act 3

- Ultimate conflict
- Climax
- Denouement

It's a simplified representation, of course. But you'll notice that Act 2 is twice as long as either Act 1 or 3. A lot of writers break up Act 2 into Acts 2a and 2b, which keeps things from getting muddled or failing to move forward in that double-length second act.

Note: This simplified representation of the three-act structure begins with the inciting incident. Most crime stories begin with the crime, which is the inciting incident. Then it establishes the hero and their everyday world. Often enough, the normal world is introduced first, as in A Game of Thrones. So, if you don't see the introduction of the world included in these examples, it's because that's implied. It's also not strictly a plot point. In other words, it doesn't change the direction of the story (from denial to investiga- tion, from investigation to hunt, from hunter to hunt- ed). Rather, the introduction of the world happens during the inciting incident or during the hero's intro-duction, which often coincides with the refusal of the call.

The hero's journey features all these components and perfectly models the three-act structure. That's why we're looking at them together, as the latter so perfectly illustrates the former. Let's try a few examples with some very com-mon stories, which most of you are already familiar with (hopefully). Remem-ber that we're only hitting on the key events of each story, the basic *plot points*. First, the hero's journey on its own:

The Hero's Journey

Act 1

- Inciting Incident: The village is imperiled (and introduced), an elixir is required

- Refusal of the call: The hero is introduced and refuses the call to retrieve the elixir, protected by a dragon

- Further complication (plot point 1): The hero's life is affected by the peril

Act 2

- Acceptance of the call: The hero sets forth on the journey to retrieve the elixir

- Border guard incident 1: A border guard tests the hero, may become an ally or spy

- Border guard incident 2: A border guard tests the hero, may become an ally or spy

- Reversal of fortune (midpoint): The hero nears the dragon's cave

- Rising conflict 1: The dragon's forces test the hero

- Rising conflict 2: The dragon's forces further test the hero

- Low point (plot point 2): The hero is laid low, failure seems certain

Act 3

- Ultimate conflict: The hero marshals his forces for a direct assault on the dragon's cave.

- Climax: The hero does direct battle with the dragon, defeating it and retrieving the elixir.

- Denouement: The hero returns to the village with the elixir and normalcy is restored.

That sounds familiar, doesn't it? It should, as 99.9% of stories are told this way. Let's take a closer look at a few examples:

The Wizard of Oz (film version)

Act 1

- Inciting Incident: Dorothy Gale has put her family farm at risk

- Refusal of the call: Dorothy flees

- Further complication (plot point 1) Dorothy is transported to Oz

Act 2

- Acceptance of the call: Dorothy must journey through Oz to return home

- Border guard incident 1: Dorothy befriends the Scarecrow, Tin Man and Lion

- Border guard incident 2: Dorothy and her allies reach the Emerald City but are refused entry

- Reversal of fortune (midpoint): To win the Wizard's favor and get home, Dorothy must retrieve the Witch's broom (the elixir)

- Rising conflict 1: The Wicked Witch of the West subdues Dorothy and her allies

- Rising conflict 2: The Witch's minions assault the allies and kidnap Dorothy

- Low point (plot point 2): Dorothy is set to die in the Witch's tower

Act 3

- Ultimate conflict: Dorothy's allies rescue her and they set off after the witch

- Climax: Dorothy and her allies face the Witch and destroy her, retrieving the elixir

- Denouement: Dorothy presents the elixir and is delivered back home, remedying her ailing village, the Gale family.

Note: The movie is really quite different to the first two Oz books, from which it is derived.

JAWS

Act 1

- Inciting Incident: The first shark attack
- Refusal of the call: The mayor disallows Brody's investigation
- Further complication (plot point 1): The second shark attack

Act 2

- Acceptance of the call: Brody tries to protect the island
- Border guard incident 1: The armada of local fishermen bring in the wrong shark
- Border guard incident 2: The third shark attack
- Reversal of fortune (midpoint): Brody heads out with his allies to hunt the shark
- Rising conflict 1: The men bicker and the shark slowly destroys the boat
- Rising conflict 2: The boat is isolated, beyond reach of help
- Low point (plot point 2): The boat is disabled and the shark is hunting them

Act 3

- Ultimate conflict: Brody loses both his allies and must face the shark alone
- Climax: Using the weapons of his allies (Quint's rifle and Hooper's air tank) Brody kills the shark
- Denouement: Brody and Hooper return to shore

Note: True, this is the film's structure, though the book also adheres to the three-act structure, with just a few variations and the notable removal of a romantic subplot.

Now let's try A Game of Thrones:

Act 1

- Inciting Incident: The King's Hand is killed

- Refusal of the call: Ned is called to replace him, but he has no wish to go

- Further complication (plot point 1): Ned learns his friend, the former hand, is dead and he sets out to solve the crime of his murder.

Act 2

- Acceptance of the call: Ned travels to the King's Castle and learns its ways

- Border guard incident 1: The King's Court resist and suspect him

- Border guard incident 2: Ned is nearly assassinated by the rival family

- Reversal of fortune (midpoint): Ned learns the mystery behind his friend's death

- Rising conflict 1: Ned instigates a new plan to avenge his friend's death and expose the guilty family

- Rising conflict 2: They strike back against Ned

- Low point (plot point 2): Ned is captured

Act 3

- Ultimate conflict: Ned has only one choice to save his remaining family

- Climax: Ned confesses to treason and is executed

- Denouement: Ned's execution reverberates through the community, creating an uprising, which continues in other stories.

True, this time the hero does not return to the village with the elixir. Or does he? Though he dies, he delivers the spirit of rebellion to the village, beginning their long and slow recovery from the peril of oppression. So in fact, the hero's journey and the three-act structure are both complete. The hero does not always survive, but the elixir of freedom is often delivered, as in such stories as the film versions of the lives and deaths of Roman slave rebel Spartacus (*Spart-acus*) and Scottish freedom fighter William Wallace (*Braveheart*).

So, what's the difference between a three-act structure and a hero's journey? The hero's journey is essentially a quest story, usually involving a journey. But this is not always so. In *One Flew Over the Cuckoo's Nest*, Randle Patrick McMurphy refuses and later accepts the call to rescue the imperiled village (the ward) by retrieving the elixir of self-respect and self-actualization, guarded by the oppressive dragon, Nurse Mildred Ratched. He faces border guards who become allies (some of the patients) or antagonists (the administration, the order- lies). Though McMurphy dies, he does succeed in freeing the men of the ward from the nurse's terrible reign.

But what about *Love Story?* The acts break down in the right places, and one could say that the hero journeys into himself, rather than outwardly into the world. The same could be argued of *Catcher in the Rye*, but it becomes harder and harder to argue as stories become more stagnant. The hero's journey becomes more metaphorical with the existentialist fiction which rose to popularity in the second half of the twentieth century. The human protagonist of Mary Shelley's Frankenstein, an existentialist tome of the highest order, is hardly a hero, and he reacts more than he acts. He certainly refuses the call to take responsibility for his creation and later the creation of the wretch's wife. And while the story breaks down into roughly three acts of appropriate length, it's hard to call it a hero's journey.

Freytag's Pyramid

Gustav Freytag's nineteenth-century pyramid dramatic structure has five parts (in this order):

- Rising Movement
- Climax
- Denouement
- Catastrophe

But don't be fooled or confused. This is really just the three-act in disguise. For Freytag, the so-called climax is, for us, the pinnacle of the hero's efforts. And that makes sense. At the midpoint of the three-act structure, the hero's skills have been tested and they are in use to the fullest. For Freytag, this is the climax of the hero's development, and everything which comes thereafter is necessarily of less importance. Though the action may rise, it is predestined from the moment of truth, which is the midpoint. This is where the so-called falling action happens, what the three-act structure thinks of as the second half of Act 2, or Act 2b. Freytag's cata- strophe is, in essence, equal to the climax of the third act in a three-act structure.

The Dan Harmond Story Circle

This is another reworking of the durable three-act structure. The *Community* creator and writer finds it easy to break the three-act structure up into eight ingredients:

- You (the hero before the journey)
- Need (a crisis, also the inciting incident)
- Go (embarking on the quest)
- Search (navigating the new world)
- Find (approaching the dragon's cave)
- Take (confront the dragon and retrieve the elixir)
- Return (deliver the elixir to save the village)
- Change (the hero is changed or improved or healed in some way)

You'll probably be able to see where the acts break. Act 1 begins with *You*, Act 2 begins with *Go*, the midpoint is Find, Act 3 begins with *Take*, and the denoue-ment is *Return/Change*.

You'll note that this change isn't included in other structures, and that's because it's classically part of character development, not plot. That's the problem with these new distortions of the three-act structure, and I've come across quite a few. Everybody puts their own twist on it, until the true structure is literally bent out of shape.

Well, he's a good sitcom writer, anyway.

The Fichtean Curve

Here is yet another way to look at the three-act structure (it is, and remains, the king of story struc- tures). The Fichtean curve is drawn like a series of waves, slowly escalating upward, like a staircase where the edges are raised, then the steps sink a bit, before rising again. Think of the stock market. It goes up quite a bit, then down a bit, then up even higher than before, only to deflate a bit and then rise higher still. Finally, the action can go no higher, it climaxes, and the arc returns to the level at which it began.

What this really tells us is that a good story has a series of crises, which should increase in intensity and all be followed by brief releases in suspense. This is re- ally more about the interplay of scenes (crises where tension rises) and sequels (where reactions to crises occur, and the tension releases just a bit). The idea is, that no good story can survive with nothing but relent- lessly increasing crises, without recalibrating a bit. But this notion is applied to the three-act structure, it does not replace it. In a good three-act story, crises escalate and are punctuat- ed by moments of temporary release.

Save the Cat

The new 'save the cat' structure breaks the three-act story arc (yup) into 15 beats:

- Opening Image – 0% to 1%
- Theme Stated – 5%
- Setup – 1% to 10%
- Catalyst – 10%

- Debate – 10% to 20%
- Break Into Two – 20%
- B Story – 22%
- Fun and Games – 20% to 50%
- Midpoint – 50%
- Bad Guys Closes In – 50% to 75%
- All is Lost – 75%
- Dark Night of the Soul – 75% to 80%
- Break Into Three – 80%
- Finale – 80% to 99%
- Final Image – 99% to 100%

Now, let's see how it correlates to the three-act structure:

Act 1

- Opening Image – 0% to 1% (introduce the village)
- Theme Stated – 5%
- Setup – 1% to 10%
- Catalyst – 10% (inciting incident)
- Debate – 10% to 20%
- Break Into Two (accepting the call)

Act 2

- B Story – 22% (border guard incident 1)
- Fun and Games – 20% to 50%
- Midpoint – 50% (reversal of fortune)
- Bad Guys Closes In – 50% to 75% (rising conflict)
- All is Lost – 75% (low point)

Act 3

- Dark Night of the Soul – 75% to 80%
- Break Into Three – 80% (ultimate conflict)
- Finale – 80% to 99% (climax)
- Final Image – 99% to 100% (denouement)

The Seven-Point Structure

The seven-point structure is yet another derivation of the three-act structure. The seven points are:

- Resolution
- Hook
- Plot turn 1
- Pinch point 1
- Midpoint
- Plot turn 2
- Pinch point 2

Here's how it correlates to the three-act structure:

- Resolution: (Climax, moved to the front of the story)
- *Act 1*
- Hook: (Inciting incident)
- Plot turn 1: (Border guard test 1)
- *Act 2*
- Pinch point 1: (Border guard test 2)
- Midpoint: (Reversal of fortune)
- Plot turn 2: (Rising conflict 1)
- Pinch point 2: (Low point)

In point of fact, stories with this structure usually begin not during the climax, but during the ulti- mate conflict, then return to it after pinch point 2 and pro-ceed to the true climax and then denoue- ment, in what is the story's traditional third act, making it more than a seven-point structure. But really, it's still just the three-act structure at its core.

They all are.

Prompts

Make a list of your favorite stories of any format. Do you clearly see the struc-ture? Outline a few and see if you can point out the three-act structure, or what-ever derivation seems right.

Exercises

Think of a book or movie you know well. (Remember that it's story structure we're dealing with, not prose technique. The foundations of structure are solid in any format and often best exemplified in film tellings.) Write down the plot points from memory, in order, to the best of your recollection.

Now go back and watch the movie, outlining every plot point as it occurs, re-peating the ones from your memory, as they happen. Take a yellow highlighter and highlight those repeated plot points, comparing them to the others you'd forgotten. Chances are, they'll be the most significant points. But examine the ones you missed. They were certainly of some importance to the plot, or they likely wouldn't be included. You may be missing similar plot points in your own story, which you can now identify and insert, as appropriate.

Now that you've got a good handle on where and when to write, what you'll write and how to outline the best structure for your story, it's time to start writing!

Almost.

5

KNOW YOUR AUDIENCE

It's an old axiom of standup comedy: Know your audience. Material that might kill in New York could die in Arizona, and what cracks them up in Tennessee could get jeers in Los Angeles. So, it's not about the material or the audience, but about pairing them correctly.

The same is true for all forms of entertainment, really (less so for non-enter-tainment art forms, such as archi- tecture, but it's still relevant). But even Leonardo da Vinci knew who his patrons were and what they wanted, be it a portrait or designs for a war machine.

So, before you write your book, give some thought to your target audience. This is crucial in a number of ways.

First, as I said earlier, you should write for yourself first and foremost (since you're the only person essentially guaranteed to read it at least once, and also if you don't want to be a pandering moneygrubber). But secondly, you must write for the intended audience. In many ways, the reader is the person of greatest consequence. Because a book without a reader is like a sound with no ears to hear it; it can hardly be said to exist at all.

There are other considerations, as well. Writing is communicating, and when communicating, it is impor- tant to be empathetic to the other person. What are their perspectives on a certain subject? How might a person be offended by what you say? If they might be entertained, how so? If you are seeking to convince, how will you gauge your effectiveness? By their reac- tions, of course. You must be empathetic to the reader in all ways. Be considerate of their time and attention. Know that the reader's eyes may tire, their time is precious. Al- ways ask yourself if the reader needs that detail or plot point. Ask yourself if it is worth their time, or if their attention won't be better spent on something more important. Will the reader remember a certain detail, if it's important? Would you rather they know it but not remember it, so that it surprises them when it crops up again later?

Know your audience in terms of what they're looking for, why they're reading your book and not somebody else's. Know your audience the same way a mu- sician knows their audience. Paul McCartney knows what his audience wants and expects from him, and he delivers. Britney Spears does the same, and so did the Sex Pistols (so never mind the, well, you know ...). John Grisham and Stephen King and Robin Cooke, JK Rowling and all the big mainstream fiction writers, know what their audiences want, and their audiences want what they deliver.

So, what do you want to deliver? What genre do you prefer? What does your audience expect from you?

The Contract with the Reader

Whatever genre you choose, whatever tastes or prefer- ences your audience may have, there are things your readers will expect. Violate these expectations and the reader will reject your book. These comprise what we call the contract with the reader, a list of rules you must abide by, in order to retain the reader's trust. Without that trust, no fictive dream can be created (as we'll see later). Here are the covenants of the contract with the reader:

Always be truthful: No matter what world your charac- ters inhabit, there are universal truths, things we know to be true. Parents will sacrifice themselves to save their children (*A Game of Thrones*), true love transcends worldly con- cerns (*Romeo & Juliet*), people have an instinct toward self-preservation (*JAWS*). These are things that are endemic to the human condition, no matter who or where those humans are. Violate these truths by having parents be indifferent to their chil- dren's fate, to their true love, or their own survival, and you are not being truthful about the way human beings are. If you are not truthful, you violate the contract with the reader, you lose the reader's trust and almost cer- tainly their time and attention.

Characters must always act at maximum capacity: A character must always choose what they feel is the best course of action. They must always be doing their very best, either in their own self-interest or in the interest of the shared cause or the greater good. For a character to slip up, just because it creates a story complication, is unacceptable. For a character to half-ass anything at all is unacceptable.

This isn't to say a character must be infallible. On the contrary; they can have misinformation, which causes them to make mistakes, or they may be physical- ly reduced and unable to function at their normal maximum capacity. But they must act at maximum capacity, given the circumstances; they must be trying their best at all times, whatever advantages or disad- vantages they may have. They must always believe they are taking the actions that will suit their goal best.

Characters must be consistent: They change, of course. This is the essence of the character arc, which we'll look at in greater detail soon. A character is apt to over- come their one fatal flaw, as Ebenezer Scrooge does so famously in A Christmas Carol. In fact, this is the rare instance of such a drastic transformation, which makes sense, because the entire story hinges on the character's flaws and the reasons for them.

But generally, a character should be true to their nature. A hardened old sea captain isn't about to walk into a scene wearing a flowery dress, without some pressing story reason, just because the writer thinks it's funny. That character wouldn't do that. A greedy man like Scrooge will not change without such a drastic inspiration for that change. It even takes four ghosts (including Marley's) to turn the old man around. I'd have changed after Marley's first words, but that's just me. Don't have a character say or do something contrary to their nature, just because it serves the story.

Establish and live by the rules of the fictive world: Different worlds can have different rules; this is the essence of fantasy fiction. In the world of the *A Quiet Place* films, errant sounds bring death from above by violent aliens. That's the rule. If somebody makes an errant sound, they must be taken by an alien. If you violate this rule even once, without a reasonable expla- nation, then the rule is false. It's not true in the context of the rules of the fictive world. You've broken that rule, so you've violated your contract with the reader.

Deliver what you promise: If you are offering a story about a dashing secret agent on a mission to save the world from the President of the United States, you are promising certain things. You promise some action (chase scenes, fight scenes), suspense (investigations and snooping around), some political over- tones, some sex appeal (the classic Bond girl is never far off), a dastardly villain with some high-tech plan (likely international in origin). You promise that there will be a final confrontation between the hero and the villain. The hero can't set off on another adventure instead. And (sorry to have to tell you this) but you promise that the hero will vanquish the villain, even if this comes at the expense of the love interest.

That rarity is likely to happen at the end as a twist, as your contract with the reader pretty much promises that the hero will save the heroine from the central conflict, the villain. If you deliver a spy thriller of this sort and kill the girl halfway through (as in the European film *Puppet on a Chain*), audiences are likely to balk (as they did in American cinemas of the 1970s). Audiences like the girl and they want to see her survive to the HEA (happily ever after) ending. Worse, if you allow the villain to prevail or for the superspy to perish, while failing to apprehend the villain, you are violating the contract with the reader. If you allow the villain to escape without presenting the climactic confrontation, you violate the contract. True, the villain may survive or mysteriously disappear without being verifiably killed, as the Joker has so many times escaped the justice of Batman. But he never ever prevails and has never killed Batman. Spoiler alert: He never will.

If you present a weepie like *Autumn in New York* or *Love Story* and the doomed character doesn't die, you've lied to your readers, and you've violated the terms of your contract. The reader is only reading the book for the sentimental experience they want to feel. Deny them that and you have cheated them and lied to them about your intentions. If you present a story about cartoon animals living in a movie studio, don't include long scenes of adults discussing their childhood abuses or alcoholism.

There are other aspects to the contract with the reader, which have to do with the protagonist and his or her relationship to the reader. We'll get more into this soon, but in brief, the protagonist is the POV (or point of view) character for the reader. The reader experiences the story through this character's eyes. Novels often have shifting POVs, from one scene to the next, but rarely change POV within a scene. Every scene has its own POV character, and that character is most often the protagonist. The connection between the reader and the protagonist, as we will see, is crucial to the fictive dream. Therefore, the protagonist can never lie to the reader, nor withhold information from the reader. Other characters may, of course, lie to the protagonist, and the protagonist may lie to another character, as long as the reader understands the lie and why it is being told. The reader and the protagonist have their own bond, their own contract, and it must never be violated. This is especially true in mysteries; if the detective reveals something the reader was not informed of, it's a cheat, it's a violation of the contract with the reader, and it's lazy writing.

Also, the reader should never know more than the protagonist, or they will jump ahead and that puts distance between the reader and the protagonist, breaking the fictive dream. There should be no daylight between the reader and the protagonist.

Never introduce characters as a narrative device. If a character appears simply to start or (worse) resolve some issue and then disappears, this is not truthful. People exist and have lives. Nobody just appears out of nowhere, at just the right time, and then vanishes, at least not in good fiction. Think of them as people, not props. Even props shouldn't be used in this way. If a prop is important, it has to be set up earlier and then paid off at the right time.

Now you know what your (or any) readership expects, let's get more specific.

Demographics

What are the demographics of your readership? If it's a legal or political thriller, it could be read by either men or women, but they're unlikely to be youths, as politics and the law are of little use or interest to teenagers. They prefer romance and fantasy. Romances are primarily written for women of various ages, but never for children. Period pieces are also enjoyed mostly by women.

What demographic are you in? Is that the demographic you want to reach? They say to write what you know, so could that be relevant here? I say to write what you know to be true (you remember). Is the inner or outer life of a person in your demographic going to be more natural for you to present truthfully? Perhaps yours is a fish out of water tale, which must include conflicting demographics, to achieve the contrast between fish and water. This is important to keep in mind, as it may affect the style of the prose, among other things.

Women tend to prefer slightly elevated writing, men seem to find it excessive. What the young adult audi- ence may find intriguing (mopey vampires), an adult audience may find ridiculous, and what some adults find enticing (millionaire bondage enthusiasts) may be repulsive or even confusing to a young readership.

Once you know your audience, let your protagonist represent them. They will see the story through the POV of the protagonist, so it will help if they identify with the protagonist on at least a few key matters.

Basically, teenage girls read about teenage girls or young women, the same for boys and young men. Adults rarely read about teenagers. The rule, basically, is that readers relate to characters their own age or just a little bit older. Too much older and they don't relate as much, which is also mostly true if the char- acter is too much younger. Child characters may be an exception to this. Generations of adult readers grew up with the Oz books, starring pre-teen Dorothy Gale, and enjoyed them in adulthood. Harry Potter has a sizeable adult readership, too, for his many adventures.

Ask yourself what books your target demographic read and enjoy. What do those books offer? How are they structured? Where do your readers spend their time? What things are you competing with for their atten- tion? A college student and a middle-aged circuit court judge are two different readerships, even if one is the child of the other.

Beyond Demographics

Put some real faces to those demographics. Picture people you know, who might be reading your books. You know them, you know how they react and what they value, what pleases and displeases them. Imagine that person reading your book and strive to please them in every way. Anticipate their harshest criticisms and correct, or even prevent, them ahead of time.

Prompts

Think of people you know, perhaps members of your family, and devise a novel especially for each one, taking their demographics and personal preferences into account. Give the stories titles, too, to get your imagination thinking about conceptual continuity and cleverness.

Exercises

Create a fictional reader, comprised of all the traits you know of, relating to their demographic. Are you writing for young parents? Let this person have ten kids. Are you writing historical American fiction? Let this person walk and talk just like John Wayne. Is your character a curious teenager with a nose for trouble? Let your imaginary reader typify the reader of such a character's adventures.

Now, let this person guide your writing decisions, in a way that is frank and forthright. No point in beating around the bush with yourself. This fictional reader is really you, so you can't be offended, not really. Separating yourself from yourself will allow you to be a bit more forthcoming about weaknesses you may not want to admit to.

Now, go online, to places where this imaginary reader might go. What books would he or she like best? If you're writing a new mobster novel, you'll find lots of online forums, filled with fans of just that. They'll be plenty forthright with their opinions, if you can take it.

Now that we know what we're writing and who we're writing it for, let's go deeper into the heart and soul of any story.

6

CHARACTERS, THE HEART AND SOUL OF THE STORY

Science fiction author, Ray Bradbury, famously said, "Plot is no more than footprints left in the snow, after your characters have run by, on their way to incredible destinations."

What he means is that characters are principle to story, even more so than plot.

But this seems counterintuitive. An espionage thriller needs a daring hero, a mystery needs an investigator, be it a plucky teen or twinkly senior citizen. Doesn't the character serve the plot? Doesn't the plot dictate who and what will best serve it? After all, JAWS is about a shark attacking an island resort town, isn't it?

No, it's not. *JAWS* is the story of a man, a police chief, who has to face his fears, in order to do his duty. He's doing a good deed (his duty) for others (the town and its people) against overwhelming odds (a killer shark in its place of power, just where the man is most vulner- able and most fearful). Stories are about people, not things. *Moby Dick* isn't about the whale, it's about the man who hunts it, Capt. Ahab. The *Oz* books take place around and about Oz, but they're about the little girl, Dorothy Gale.

The Exorcist is much more about the people than the demon, who only serves to bring each character's secrets out into the open, preying on their lingering guilt and doubt, the twin enemies of faith. This is evident more so in the book than the film, but one by one, the demon torments each person in the house with their own inse- curities. Beyond Father Damien Karras' personal crisis of faith, a man torn between faith and science (albeit the soft science of psychology), the story focuses on the little girl's mother's guilt over her failed marriage to Regan's absent father. The mother's valet has a shadowy WWII past, her daughter's caretaker harbors lust for Karras. These aren't just frightened people in a haunted house. They are given life by detail, and these details help to reinforce the theme of the story, a concept we'll discuss later.

True, certain stories require certain types of characters, but these characters must transcend their tropes; they must be more than narrative devices to deliver the thrills and chills of the plot. James Bond is a three- dimensional character (more so in the books than the films). He drinks to excess, he's haunted by demons of personal loss and advancing age. He's more than just the world's most dangerous and most well-endowed playboy ("Oh, James," indeed).

Before we move forward, let's get some terminology straight. A protagonist is the character who strives toward the story's main goal. An antagonist stands in direct opposition to the protagonist's goal. Every story has a story goal, and each scene has a smaller goal, which must be accomplished, in order for the main goal to be achieved.

In a scene, a character strives actively toward a goal, meets with conflict, and endures a setback or disaster. In a sequel, a character experiences emotion (from the previous conflict), thought (about the next action to be taken) and decision (establishing the next course of action). Every scene and sequel has a protagonist, often but not always the story's main protagonist. In order to remain allied with the protagonist, the reader must find that protagonist compelling; they must desire to be in the protagonist's company.

This brings me back to an axiom I used earlier, and one I stand by. The equation for a good story is this: A like- able person doing a good deed for others, against over- whelming odds. Right now, we're concerned with the first part of that equation, the likeable person.

The Likeable Character

The first thing to know is that, if you're writing a story of redemption, you will be chasing up a blind alley, if you use the *Christmas Carol* method of slow-turning an unlikeable character into a likeable one.

First of all, it's been done. This venerable tale has been told countless times and will go on being retold. Why?

Because it works. A good execution of this story is compelling fiction, the like of which rarely occurs today. It's so well-known that all you or anybody can do is to ape it, to copy it, to steal it. But we all know this story.

Second, this story was written in another era, and the times have drastically changed. Storytelling conven- tions have changed. Everything about our society has changed, and radically so. Nobody wants to spend two hours (or two minutes) with a loudmouthed, hateful character like Holden Caulfield, the bitter malcontent from *A Catcher in the Rye*. And nobody is going to invest their valuable time waiting around for a bitter pill to sweeten up. In Dickens' time, there was little else to do for recreation, and people had longer attention spans. Now, two hours is more valuable than it used to be, and nobody's interested in wasting a moment of it. A good writer is empathetic toward their audience and knows their time is valuable.

Think of it this way: A book is like a party, and the characters are all guests. The writer, the party's host, invites the reader to attend the party. A good host has guests who may disagree, who are colorful, who may not be to everybody's taste. That's life. But imagine you show up to this party and it's entirely dominated by an unlikeable, charmless, crude, miserable, aggressive, sloppy, bitter jerk. The host assures you that he gets better as the story goes on, but you have to stay till the end of the party to find that out. In the meantime, you've got to stand around and endure this person acting out. The other guests hardly have a chance to get your attention.

Is that the kind of party you want to throw? Is this a guest you would invite to your party? No.

Likeable can mean many things. Nobody likes a person who is too perfect. They're just not real, not relatable. It's a mistake that creates bland, two-dimensional char- acters. And it's not truthful, because nobody is perfect. If you're not truthful, you are violating your contract with the reader.

Note the equation does not specify a virtuous person, a heroic person, an attractive person. It specifies that the person is likeable. But what does that mean? Surely, it's subjective, according to varying tastes. What one person finds likeable, others may find repulsive.

Clearly, you can't please everybody all the time. No writer ever does or ever will. You have to please your- self. So, ask yourself what qualities you find likeable in a person. They may include:

- Wit

- Intelligence

- Empathy

- Honesty

- Courage

- Self-control

- Physical attractiveness

- Being fun to be around

- Wealthy

- Powerful

- Charming

But a likeable person needn't have all these qualities. They might, but that's a pretty high bar and excludes a lot of potentially likeable characters. These are the qualities of the hero.

Three Types of Heroes

Without getting too deep into history or theory, every writer has to know the three most common types of heroes. Joseph Campbell gives us more, but these are the three you will come across most often. In constructing our protagonist (and his or her allies), it's important to know what kind of hero you're creating.

The three types we're concerned with here are: the willing hero, the unwilling hero, and the existential hero.

The willing hero comes to us, courtesy of Ancient Greek and Rome, which collectively give us Hercules, a demigod. Born with great strength, but tricked into a rueful act, Hercules sets about achieving great tasks, which he does willingly to atone for his sins. He is strong, clever, capable, and willing. In fact, the word *hero* derives from the name *Hercules*.

The unwilling hero has no personal need for heroics, and no desire to be heroic. He or she does not seek out adventure. He or she has no great strengths or gifts for heroic pursuits. They are common in their world. But when called upon, and only after staunch refusal, they answer the call and draw upon hidden strengths in battle. Tolkien's Hobbits are such unwilling heroes.

The existential hero fights personal battles, willingly or unwillingly. This character has the hero's strength, but they fight the battle within. They seek not to conquer the world or defeat a foe, but to understand it. This character is often driven by rue, like the willing hero. But they seek peace and often solitude, like the unwilling hero. The existential hero addresses ques- tions of identity and meaning. Whether they succeed in answering these questions is secondary, but it does determine whether they become an existential hero who comes to their own conclusions (Ernest Hemingway's Nick Drake) or an existential villain who allows society to come to these conclusions and then abides by them (Mary Shelley's Wretch from *Frankenstein*).

Which hero serves your story best? Which hero type will shape the story most effectively?

The Anti-Hero

But just as likeable as any hero, is the anti-hero. The hero may be described as a character, who does the right thing because they embody the right. The anti-hero does the right thing, despite embodying the wrong. Superman is a hero, the living personification of truth, justice, and the American way. Batman is an antihero, a controversial vigilante, who acts outside of and above the law, leaving a trail of blood and broken bones, a tormented psychotic. Nevertheless, he is a force of good.

Dickens' Oliver Twist is a hero, a blameless orphaned child, struggling to survive. Ebenezer Scrooge is an anti-hero; he is heartless greed personified.

American films gave us director Frank Kapra's visions of heroic everyday citizens. Films like *Casablanca* gave us darker, conflicted citizens, for whom the right thing goes against every reasonable circumstance other than an inborn natural impulse, however foreign it may feel to the hero.

After *Casablanca*, the anti-hero rose in popular fiction. Of course, anti-heroes date as far back as the bible (David, Elijah, and Jesus were just three men who rebelled against the establishment for the greater good, though they were labelled insurrectionists, rebels, and criminals). Fiction gave us Robin Hood, a man who did the right thing (giving to the poor) despite embodying the wrong thing (a rogue agent, a criminal against the established authority).

The tradition of the American Western demonstrated the shift from heroic characters (*High Noon*) to anti- heroes (*The Searchers*) to comedic anti-heroes like Butch Cassidy and the Sundance Kid. Gangster films, from *Angels with Dirty Faces* to *The Godfather* novel and films, have also given us the rise of the criminal anti-hero.

How can a criminal become an anti-hero? First of all, anti-heroes often exhibit the qualities of the hero. They have the wit, the intelligence, the courage. The anti- hero, like the hero, lives by their own code and they stick to it. They're honest about who and what they are. They have integrity. They have empathy. They don't live by society's rules, but that's because society often lives by corrupted rules. The anti-hero is truly the embodiment of good in these cases, and the established authority is the true evil. These are the stories of people like Spartacus, like French safecracker Henri *Papillon* Cherierre.

By comparison, those whom the anti-hero comes up against lack these qualities. They may be members of society, or other outsiders who lack the anti-hero's empathy and integrity. But they are likely to be humor- less, dim, selfish, cowardly, dishonest, perhaps wealthy and powerful.

This brings us to the phenomenon of relative morality. The anti-hero is likeable, often because he or she is so much better than the characters around them. True, Batman is a menace, but he's better than the Joker. Richard Blaine may be a gunrunner and a gambler and a drunk, but he's not corrupt. He is secretly generous with the needy who pass through Rick's Café American. He may be selfish, but he's honest about it. He lives by his own code, with his integrity intact. And he does the right thing, against every practical impulse other than his own innate morality, which even he cannot deny.

And there is scarcely a more likeable character in all of Casablanca or all of film.

If you're writing a comedy, know this: Comedy is the realm of the anti-hero. The comedic hero is, by nature, an anti-hero. He or she is an outsider, a have-not, a slob, who goes up against the snob. Comedy is the poor person's revenge. Charlie Chaplin's little tramp is just that; a tramp. He has nothing. But with the love of humanity in his heart, his wiles and his innate moral compass, he transcends the poverty of his surround- ings, time and again. He may or may not become wealthy, but he always is rewarded with richness of spirit, with contentment, with love.

From the Marx Brothers to Bugs Bunny to Mr. Bean, comedic heroes are every-man characters, forced by circumstance to rise above. This tradition includes modern incarnations, like Homer Simpson or Bojack Horseman.

The Complex Character

Whatever type of hero you prefer or desire, whichever you feel will best serve or shape your story, the charac- ters must be complex. Not only your protagonist, but your antagonist, your allies, as many characters as you feel your reader can digest, should be complex.

This is surprisingly simple to accomplish. The first thing to remember is, as we discussed, characters should not be narrative devices to further a story. True, the story has its own requirements, but so does the character and so does the reader.

The complex character is both ordinary and extraordinary. Hercules himself was born to a mortal woman and the king of the gods (half ordinary, half extraordinary). Herman Melville's Billy Budd is a common merchant seaman, but he has extraordinary qualities, which affect the other men and overturn events aboard *The Rights of Man.*

A complex character is a three-dimensional character. And I don't mean to be esoteric about some nebulous third dimension. I mean, a good character has three aspects, three dimensions to their character.

A good protagonist, for example, will have three quali- ties; two good, one bad. Let your protagonist have a flaw, something about them that makes them human. Let your protagonist be honest, courageous, but sloppy. Consider letting them be handsome, clever, but phobic. Because nobody is all good or all bad. This humanizes our characters, making them more relatable to your readers. Your readers aren't perfect, after all. And if they're to create a bond with your protagonist, your protagonist should likewise not be perfect.

Cyrano de Bergerac is a skilled swordsman and poet, but he is wracked with insecurity over his appearance.

Christian de Neuvillette is handsome, courageous, but insecure over his lack of eloquence.

Note that one of these general qualities includes a skill or strength or talent of some kind, something which makes them suited to the task. Michael Corleone is a war hero, so he's capable of the tasks before him. Cyrano is a feared swordsman. They're good at what they do, and that skill proves useful on their journey.

A good antagonist should also be balanced. Nobody is all good, and nobody is all bad. While your protagonist may have two good qualities and one bad, give your antagonist two bad qualities and one good. Let your antagonist be powerful, wealthy, but dedicated to nature (as many supervillains have been). Let your antagonist be ill-tempered, vindictive, but with inordi- nate empathy for children or animals.

Cyrano's antagonist, the Comte de Guiche, is entitled, petty, but ultimately shows courage and humility.

Let your allies have conflicting traits as well. Should your object of romantic desire be the perfect man or woman? No. Let your love interest be attractive, intelli- gent, but quick-tempered. Let another ally be brilliant with high tech, dedicated to the cause of good, but also a womanizer.

The Conflicted Character

Complex characters will also be prone to internal conflict. Michael Corleone, of The Godfather, for exam- ple. Michael's three qualities are cleverness, courage, and ruthlessness. These characteristics made him a war hero. They also put him on a track, moving away from his family and their criminal empire. He seeks to live a life free of it, as he tells his girlfriend, Kaye, early on. But his loyalty to his family, who are besieged by their enemies, creates a conflict within him. He is torn between his own desires for a new life, and his duty to his old life. He's conflicted.

Martin Brody, a willing hero who is dutiful, honest, but secretly fearful, moved to Amity Island from New York for a safer, more tranquil life for his family. He is also deathly afraid of the water. His duty calls upon him to face those fears and throw his life once more into peril, two things he does not want to do. But he has no choice. He's conflicted.

Romeo and Juliet are torn between their love for one another and their duties to their families, whom they love. They're conflicted. Hamlet is torn between his love of his mother and his creeping realization that she was in part to blame for his beloved father's death. He's conflicted ... and of course quite melancholy. Who wouldn't be?

Cyrano is conflicted by his own desire for Roxanne and his efforts to prove himself worthy of her by winning her heart for Christian, whom he knows is not really worthy of her. He's terribly conflicted.

Conflicted characters feel pain, another crucial aspect of a good character. Hercules felt remorse for killing his wife and daughters (though he was under a spell at the time). Bruce Wayne still feels the pain of being unable to protect his beloved parents. Michael Corleone loves his family too much to abandon them. When his father is nearly killed, pain drives Michael to abandon his own ideals. Captain Veer, of The Rights of Man, is conflicted between his duty to the law, the ramifications of his actions aboard his ship, and his feelings for innocent, luckless Billy Budd. He cannot free the boy, as he would like, and still fulfil his duty to the crown.

These are characters who reverberate through time, whose stories connect to readers and viewers, genera- tion in and generation out. Seek to create characters of this sort, and you will reach out to people for years far outreaching your own. Fail to do this, and you won't.

Tips and Tricks

- Take care in constructing the right name for your characters. Ugly characters have ugly names.

- Give each character a distinct voice or vocal tick, such as answering questions with questions or using phrases like *per se* or *get me?* (though this shouldn't be overused, or they'll become annoying caricatures).

- If they don't have a vocal tick, give them a mannerism, like scratching their nose.

- Know every character's motivation.

- Give each character a backstory, even if it never comes up in the actual story.

Prompts

If you're stuck on developing a character, think of somebody you know and make a few tweaks to make them unrecognizable. They'll still be recognizable to you; then let them act in your fictive situation the way they would in real life ... and at maximum capacity, of course.

If that doesn't work, try going to the phone book or other directory and selecting five names at random. Now write descriptions for them, based on their names alone. This will get the brain thinking in terms of developing characters.

Exercises

Describe a character from head to toe. Make a list starting like this one:

- Head:
- Neck:
- Shoulders:

- Chest:
- Arms:

Now fill that list in with five things for the head and two for everything else. This will help you envision your character and it will give them added life and vibrancy in your imagination.

Another good exercise is to dress each character. Do what you did above, but describe only the clothes they wear. This will also help bring the character to life.

Reverse this exercise by picking a set of clothes (wed- ding finery, ranch wear, threadbare rags) and describe the kind of person who might wear those clothes. Describe them in terms of their character or personal- ity, not their appearance.

Here's a good exercise for writing emotion. Pick an emotion and write about a person experiencing it. Make it one long paragraph. But tailor the words and style to reflect the emotion. Is the person fearful? Use words which relate to fear. Is the person comfortable and relaxed? Use long sentences and flowing words. Is the person panicked? Try short words and incomplete sentences. Imagine the character in that emotional state is doing the writing. This will give them a voice.

A good way to characterize someone is by how others react to them. If they are fearful, the character may be frightening. If others are impressed, the character is likely to be impressive. So make a list of reactions, of impressions, and then draw a character based on these impressions.

Now that we've got our characters and our plot, the *who* and the *what,* let's turn our attention to the *where.*

Setting.

7

A WHOLE NEW WORLD …
AND HOW TO BUILD IT

When we think about setting, we often think of world-building, and this makes perfect sense. When you write longform fiction, the novel in particu- lar, you are engaging in world-building. But this is not as straight-for- ward as it may seem.

First of all, world-building has three distinct forms. It involves the actu- al creation of a new world, as one may do in fantasy fiction of any sort. But world-building involves more than that, as we'll soon see.

Setting as Character

First of all, it's important to understand where the world of the story fits in to the machinery of story, what functions it can serve. Of course, setting is important, as it gives the characters some place to be.

And while setting is crucial to a good story, well told, it also serves the story as it is chosen, like characters, for its appropriateness to the story. If yours is a horror story or perhaps a mystery, an isolated location is best. This is because these stories require a vortex, which keeps the characters locked in the conflict, with no choice but to resolve it. There can be no escape. This is why so many old horror movies occurred in isolated mansions on stormy nights, which also brought down any communications. Any version of *The Cat and the Canary* uses this device, as do the mysteries of Agatha Christie (*Murder on the Orient Express*). Dracula movies generally take place in his isolated castle. *The Shining's* Overlook Hotel is just such a location, under just such circumstances.

If your story is a coming-of-age story, you may choose a bucolic small town, where so many people do come of age. A political thriller will likely take your characters to the world centers of power. A maritime adventure is almost certain to take place at sea.

But setting also reflects the characters. Internal turmoil may be illustrated by a storm, which rises during the conflict. A tranquil setting may take on a monstrous aspect to reflect the lives of those inside it. We see both of these in both the movie and book versions of *The Shining.*

And, as with the Overlook Hotel, a setting can take on a character of its own. Gabriel Garcia Marquez's fictional Columbian town, Sucre, in *A Chronicle of a Death Foretold*, is ultimately the identifiable character respon- sible for the victim's murder. There may be no better example than the end of the same author's One Hundred *Years of Solitude*, but I will not give that away here.

Shadowy, gritty characters like private eyes, inhabit the shadowy, gritty settings of urban life, where the crimes they investigate might happen. Surrealistic hellscapes are where dream villains like Freddie Kreuger do their best work.

But it's not all gloom and doom. Settings can have a positive, restorative effect on people, as can be seen in so many romance novels, which take place in woodland lodges that somehow help visitors overcome their diffi- culties. This is a common approach in magical realism, in which a real-world setting still has vaguely magical components.

Settings also reflect the inner lives of their inhabitants, which makes them crucial to their characterizations. In this and other ways, setting and character go hand-in- hand. You know what kind of man Scrooge is by how he lives, alone in a mansion. You learn just as much about the modest but filled homes of his employee and his nephew. You know what kind of people live and work in Mayberry, USA, just by looking at the streets. It's notable that the word Mayberry has itself become synonymous with a quiet, American small town.

Fantasy World-Building

Fantasy worlds require intense world-building. Like real world-building, detail is required, and authenticity and consistency are vital. But in a fantasy world, unlike the real world, little can be taken for granted. Things can be likened to touchstone objects, like cars or houses or guns. But in a fantasy world, there is likely to be a foreign language. There will be creatures for which there are real-world parallels, such as a creature with the body of a horse but the neck and head of an ostrich, but it will have a different name. Everything will. Weapons will be different and have to be described in most cases. The more fantastical the world is, the more this will have to be done.

This brings us to another axiom: In the particular lay the universal, this world, like the real world, will have particularities. They won't be the same, but there must be particularities, details. And, as in the real world, they must be consistent. Here, more than anywhere, you must commit to your contract with the reader, as you create the rules of the world and then rigorously stick to them. They must be consistent. Whether yours is a sunny, colorful world of lollypop forests and butterfly monarchs, or a mountainous jungle buried deep beneath the Earth, it must be consistent to be real.

Remember that setting includes weather. There will be weather consistencies, which are informed by the setting, the story, the characters. Sam Spade's foggy surroundings perfectly suit the detective's lifestyle and character, so it made a perfect choice for Dashiell Hammett. Mayberry is invariably sunny. A rugged coastal setting is likely to invite stormy weather. So your fantasy world must have weather currents, seasons, other things which make it real. These must be consistent.

Real World-Building

Building a world in a non-fantasy novel, in other words rendering a real-world setting, offers a few advantages. Less detail is required, because fewer new things need to be introduced. Readers already know certain things. Details are still necessary, as we'll soon see, but less explanation is usually necessary.

Real-world stories may still (and often do) take charac- ters to the far reaches of the globe. From the Amazon rainforest to the winding streets of Rome to the halls of power in Washington DC, you may be compelled to render real-world environments, which have their own details, their own specifics. You must re- search these thoroughly.

And it goes beyond the city streets and other land- marks. Different locations affect people differently. Citizens of the US capital tend to be charming, but not forthcoming. Parisians can be particularly snobbish, but this is not so of those in the South of France. Any urban setting will make its inhabitants more guarded in some cases, more aggressive in others. Inhabitants of small towns in Greece may be very welcoming of strangers, which is cultural.

Weather and season are still important, as well. And, as in any fantasy world, there have to be elements that make the action possible. A duel of paranormal shapeshifting creatures needs plenty of room to fight, without attracting the attention of the entire city. If a city's involvement is necessary to the story, the location must be near enough to that city.

Where real world-building becomes more challenging, is when you are rendering a historical fiction piece, such as a Regency romance. Here, details of clothing and fashion and contemporary technology can be just as foreign as anything in any far away fantasy land. But the details must be consistent. Technological limita- tions of time and location must be strictly adhered to. This includes how many bullets a pistol can hold in any given year, whether or not your character might actu- ally be wearing shoes or not (often not, by the way).

Weather and season are crucial to such pieces. Westerns almost always occur in a remote or isolated location, which makes sense, because the American landscape of the era was much less densely populated than it is now. Almost anywhere you went in the 1800s American West, you were still somewhat isolated. Weather is vital to bringing these settings alive. Rain and snow storms, brutal heat and drought, sandstorms and earthquakes and flashfloods are all good sources of man-against- nature conflict and can do a lot to build up suspense and tension.

Often the Twain Shall Meet

Worthy of note here is building the world which is both fantastical and yet familiar, and this is the land of the dystopian future. These worlds are inhabited by things we know and can already name. But something about the world has changed radically. The world may be plunged into silence and stillness, to avoid brutal death from above, as in the *A Quiet Place* films. The world could be in ruins, run by organized, speaking apes, which keep the primitive human population enslaved, as in the original novel *Planet of the Apes* (written and published in French in 1963). It could be the ultra- urban cityscape of *Bladerunner*. Here, new details mix with old. Some things can be taken for granted, other things must be recreated to show the advance of time. This is part of the attraction of dystopian fiction.

Steam-punk is another genre which mixes the known and the unknown, using Nineteenth-century tech- nology in unusual and inventive ways.

Examples of World-Building

J.R.R. Tolkien's The *Hobbit* gave him the chance to create an intricate new world, Middle Earth, filled with specific communities, which are human-like, but which also present fanciful locales and objects. While the story structure is firmly in the hero's journey wheel- house, the world seems completely new and fresh (though it looks a lot like New Zealand).

The world is influenced strongly by Norse mythology, rooting it in the real world, at least by association. It is Middle Earth, not Middle Venus.

Weather and season are both Earthlike, but the time is distinctly pre-human (by something like 6,000 years), fully removing it from modern society.

A *Game of Thrones* is comparable, giving us a vaguely historical setting, in a land based on human history. Its characters are human, its setting is essentially human … with dragons.

But *A Game of Thrones* and *The Hobbit* inhabit worlds which are very familiar, rooted in human history. From the craggy Anglo mountains of Westeros and Essos to the steamy jungles of Middle Earth, these are places we already know and understand.

Likewise, the urban world of *Bladerunner,* which goes into the future to build its world. Once again, it is rooted in our shared human experience (the location is Los Angeles, California). And while the technology is advanced, it's all quite recognizable. Just as A Game of Thrones is rural England with dragons, Bladerunner is basically Los Angeles with robots.

These worlds all seem foreign and fantastic, yet they are actually quite familiar to us. So when you make your world, consider your reader's associations with the world they know. Does it make sense to create a new world where nothing is as it is on Earth? Could a human even exist in such an environment? Why would a human be valuable to such an environment? These questions can all be answered, of course. But as the writer, you'll have to answer them.

The *Invisible Life of Addie LaRue* author, V.E. Schwab, builds her worlds from a characters-first point of view, beginning with the character's most central values.

Award-winning *The Handmaid's Tale* author, Margaret Atwood, reportedly builds her worlds first, by imag- ining how her character might eat breakfast. The details of how the character prepares food, the tools and kitchen, touches off something in the writer. It reveals the economy of the setting, the location based on what is available, what the social structures of that world are.

Chuck Wendig wrote his Wanderers settings by focusing on his plot and characters. The writer is quoted as saying, "The world serves the story, the story doesn't serve the world."

Tips and Tricks

- Study other writers: Read their articles, their books, study the words they create.

- Decide where to start: Where in the setting's history does your story take place?

- Combine different worlds: Casablanca and High Noon have been re- told in outer space countless times.

- List Laws and Rules: In television series slang, this is called the show's bible. It lists all the details of setting and character, which must be consistent. It can't all be committed to memory and should be written down and well- organized.

- Draw a map: The bigger the setting, the more regions will be necessary. Map them so your references to direction will be consistent and correct.

- List flora and fauna: Part of the bible of your new world.

- Utilize senses: Details which can't be overlooked, as we'll soon see.

- Reflect the world's values: Setting can serve the story and also shape it. Setting both influences the values of its inhabitants, and it reflects them.

- Explore thematic elements: We'll get more into theme shortly.

Prompts

If you're stuck building your world, think of the worlds of your favorite books, the worlds in the genre you've chosen, the worlds your readers expect. Think of the places you lived during the best times of your life, and the worst times of your life. Think of where you live now, and where you'd rather live. Why? What associa- tions are there from the environment and the events in your life?

Exercises

Consider the tone of the world you're building. Is it the Great Depression of the 1930s or the swinging sixties in London, England? Is it a distant planet or a distant time? Start by writing down the details that result from the setting:

- Clothing
- Technology
- Slang
- Food
- Climate
- Geography

You'll find that the details start with the characters, the things they wear and eat and say, but these things will invariably be related to the environment, the time, the setting. Make this list as long as you can or as long as you wish. Keep the material for your new book's bible, containing all such world details.

Now, let's move on to the things which inspire this world and its inhabitants and the writer who creates both.

Themes.

8

ENRICHING THE NARRATIVE:
A GUIDE TO THEMES

Theme is an oft-overlooked aspect of storytelling. A lot of writers have a hard enough time with dialogue, setting, and other aspects of storytelling. But theme remains vital to good storytelling.

Theme can seem small, even insignificant. But think of theme as the very tip of an arrow. True, it's hard to see. But it is at the forefront of the whole device. It's the reason the thing exists at all, in fact. The entire purpose of an arrow is to deliver the sharp point at its tip. The entire purpose of fiction is to deliver the sharp point at its core, the theme.

Theme is often referred to as *premise*, though this can be confusing. Premise can be confused for concept. But a concept is the idea the story is designed to bring to life, and we've already gone over that. The premise is the lesson, the point the story is trying to bring to life.

First of all, it's noteworthy that just about any story naturally has a premise, or a theme, by the very nature of its existence. We, as readers, can draw a conclusion from just about any set of fictive circumstances.

For example, in *Fifty Shades of Grey*, Christian Grey offers lust to open up the world of Anastasia Steele, but she offers the love he truly craves. It can be said, there- fore, that this story tells us that love is a greater force than lust, because this is what happens in the story; the story demonstrates this.

Stories like those in the *Lord of the Rings* books tell us that even the most unlikely spirit can be heroic, in times of great need. It's not much of a theme, but it's enduring, flexible and very common.

Theme is often eschewed altogether, especially in romance fiction. It may be incidentally there, but it is not developed or even intentional. But the further back one goes, the more theme is evident in good story- telling. In fact, the more fiction subjugates itself to the tyranny of the premise.

This phrase means just what it would seem to mean; that everything serves the premise. Instead of being incidental, theme is at the center of every character, every detail. The arrow that finds its mark, flies in a single direction, always behind the very tip, always serving the premise. Everything about the arrow is merely a delivery system for its very tip.

Much of Charles Dickens' work presents the theme of moral and social decrepitude, as in *A Christmas Carol* or *Oliver Twist*. His premise was often that England was failing its imperiled populace, that the empire was waning, and that action was needed by the rich (like Scrooge) to help the poor (like Oliver), to reverse the country's decline. Every character plays its part to prove these premises.

Religion is a common theme in fiction. Herman Melville's work was very thematic. His epic Moby Dick has several themes, in fact. Notably, it's a lesson about the futility of revenge. Captain Ahab loses his leg to the white whale, which he pursues, to his own demise. This is what happens; this is the premise, which is proven by the events. But Moby Dick is also a story of man's hubris. Ahab is arrogant, representing the human race, which believes it can control nature, that it is the master of the Earth. But for Melville, a devoutly reli- gious man, this was man assuming the role of God. His story proves the folly of that lack of humility.

His *Billy Budd, Foretopman*, is a parable of the passion of the Christ. This is an- other common theme in fiction. What we learn from stories in this tradition is that indi- vidual sacrifice for the greater good is often necessary and always di- vine. It's a simple matter of recasting the major elements. Instead of Jerusalem, the setting is *The Rights of Man*, a Nineteenth-century naval ship. Innocent sail- or, Billy Budd, is the Christ figure, while conflicted Capt. Vere substitutes for Pontius Pilate. Master at Arms Claggart represents the Pharisees, whose power is threatened by the new force, who is even then gathering his apostles (the other sailors) and influencing the entire populace (the crew and the officers).

This story, with its inherent premise, is oft-told. *One Flew Over the Cuckoo's Nest* is a passion parable, as are the American films *Cool Hand Luke* and *Spartacus*.

It's interesting to note that *Billy Budd*, Foretopman, is often interpreted as having a homosexual theme, with its references to Billy's handsomeness and explaining Claggart's driving emotion as homosexual frustration. But to un- derstand a story's theme, one must under- stand the author. Interpretations can be subjective, but the facts surrounding the life of the author are objec- tive. In this case, Melville was both a seaman and a Christian, with no evidence of homosexuality in his life at all, despite conjecture to the contrary.

Hundreds of years earlier, Shakespeare also wrote heavily thematic work. His *Romeo and Juliet*, perhaps the most often-retold story ever, tells us that love pre- vails over hate, as this is what happens in the story. The titular teenagers may not survive their travail, but their families learn the painful lesson of their toxic hatred and set off on a new course, as a result of the kids' sacrifice.

Othello tells us, on the other hand, that suspicion can undo even the truest love. The play also tells us that dishonesty leads to ruin, as the fate of Iago demonstrates. *Titus Andronicus* imparts the theme of social responsibility. Titus is offered leadership and declines, and his life and family end in ruin.

Though the theme can be central to a story, and is often intentional, it is even more common that a theme emerges in the writing. It's the clever writer who can recognize it and let it grow, let it subtly influence the plot, characters, and dialogue.

Existentialism was a common theme of fiction throughout the Twentieth century (and just before), coinciding with the rise of this distinctly modern philosophy, which focuses on individual identity. Characters who take the internal journey to discover who and what they truly are, and where they belong in society, are existential characters. Those who answer these questions for themselves, like Hemingway's Nick Drake, are existential heroes. Those who fail and allow society to define them, like Mary Shelley's Wretch in *Frankenstein*, are existential villains.

A few modern examples come to us from the exem- plary novels of the Twentieth century. To wit:

- THE GODFATHER: The individual is indivisible from the community
- THE EXORCIST: Faith is greater than knowledge
- JAWS: Duty usurps personal desire
- THE LORD OF THE RINGS: Power corrupts
- ONE HUNDRED YEARS OF SOLITUDE: Isolation leads to destruction
- LOVE STORY: Life is precious and fleeting
- CRIME AND PUNISHMENT: Morality is circumstantial
- THE NOTEBOOK: Love and loss often go hand-in-hand

So, while you can write a book where the theme is inci- dental, you can also go out of your way to let a theme rise to the surface, to accentuate it and let it add an extra, memorable layer to your novel or other piece of longform fiction.

Themes help us to better understand ourselves, our lives, our world.

Tips and Tricks

When choosing and developing your themes, here are some things to keep in mind:

- Be honest: Don't try to prove a premise you don't believe. Don't pander to the reader.

- Be timely: Social satire, like that of Dickens, can resonate generations later, as his does.

- Be kind: Let your theme reflect hopefulness, a way to improve the human condition.

- Be subtle: Don't spoon-feed your readers. Theme is a show-don't-tell proposition.

- Be deliberate: Themes that are incidental should still be clear.

- Be dutiful: If you're serving the theme, do not contradict it. Everything serves the tyranny of the premise, especially the writer.

- Be clear: Identify the theme, to yourself, if not to your readers.

- Be open: You may discover more than one theme in your novel. Good. Develop them all.

- Be confident: You may not know your theme when you start. Good. Don't let not knowing the theme prevent you from writing.

- Be clever: Use symbolism and motifs (recurring images) to impart your theme.

Prompts

If you're having trouble thinking of a theme, but don't wish to write without one, just think of things your parents taught you. They might include:

- If you want something, you have to go for it.

- You'll only regret the things you don't do.

- The needs of the many outweigh the needs of the few.

- Do unto others as you would have others do unto you.

- Might doesn't make right.

Make a list of a few from your own experience!

Exercises

Take one story you're familiar with and consider the theme. Write it out in as much detail as one sentence will allow. Now do it with as many stories as you know well.

Take any one of the stories you just analyzed. Write a list of the motifs in that story. If the story is *The Lord of the Rings*, you may choose prizes, challenges, quests, friends, enemies, life, death, greed, corruption, etc. Now think of different ways you can visually impart those motifs. Consider character names, weather and season, as good ways to put these motifs across.

Now that we've got a good handle on theme, let's move on to the best ways of making that theme, and every- thing else in your story, come more fully to life.

Description.

9

THE ART OF SHOWING, NOT TELLING

 "Don't tell me the moon is shining; show me the glint of light on broken glass."

— ANTON CHEKHOV (VANKA)

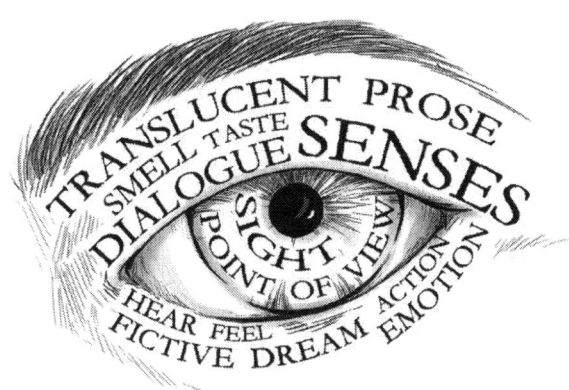

Show, don't tell. This is common advice to writers, and it's good advice. But it can be a little misleading.

First of all, the adage should be amended to 'show and tell'. Sometimes, you need to show, sometimes it's better to tell. But first, let's talk about the difference between the two. It's not as clear as you may think.

The idea of 'show, don't tell' is to take the author out of the experience as much as possible, to put the reader in the heart of the action.

Translucent vs. Transparent Prose

First, let's talk a bit about prose, which is the narrative part of the story (not the dialogue). Here is where much (but not all) of the descriptive work in a novel or other piece of longform fiction will be found.

In general, good prose is clear and concise. All good writing comes down to these things. If it's not clear, it fails to communicate. If it's not concise, then it's redun- dant and, frankly, probably not clear.

So, modern fiction doesn't use a lot of elevated language, as it did in centuries past. It also avoids the overly stylized voices made popular by the likes of Hunter S. Thompson or Charles Bukowski. Good prose supports the action; it presents it, it doesn't stand in front of it or dominate it.

So, it came to be said that good prose was transparent. It didn't get in the way, it was essentially invisible. This is the style-free type of prose, which propels modern page-turners. The author and the reader disappear, the action and the characters and the story get all the attention.

But let's take a moment to reconsider. Good prose should not be truly transparent, as this can result in bland writing. Instead, the prose should be translucent. It should not obscure the action, but it should tint it in a certain way. Think of it as good lighting in a film; it tells the story, without drawing attention to itself. But the lighting in a horror movie will be different from the lighting in a cartoon musical film for children. Lighting evokes mood and can affirm theme, and so can prose.

So, if you're writing the story of a hard-nosed PI, your prose is likely to reflect that character, his or her way of thinking or speaking. Using shorter words, more frank expressions, would set the tone for a story taking place in that world. Westerns and other period pieces may use longer sentences, words more particular to the period, including verbs and nouns, which are no longer in vogue. They were in vogue then, and using them in descriptions can make the period come to life.

Translucent prose will make the fictive dream all the more powerful and vibrant to the reader.

The Fictive Dream

We've discussed this before, and here is where it really comes into play. We've talked about the protagonist as the POV, or point-of-view, character. This is the char- acter who serves as the surrogate for the reader. The reader sees his- or herself in the role of the protagonist. For all intents and purposes, the POV character is the reader.

For many years, the POV character was not the protag- onist. Think of *Moby Dick*, told by a low-ranking sailor, Ishmael, who observes the action and relays it to the reader. Frankenstein is told in this fashion as well. But the second-person perspective is pretty much dead. The twenty- and twenty-first centuries feature either first-person or third-person POVs.

For creating the fictive dream, the third-person limited omniscient perspective is best. This is because there is no buffer between the reader and the character. Even in first person, there is that narrative voice between the reader and the action. The character is telling the reader what is happening in first person (I walked through the door) instead of showing the reader what is happening in third person (he walked through the door). Because in third person, the *he* is really the reader. In first, it's the character.

The fictive dream, you'll recall, is the sense that the action is happening right in front of the reader's eyes and ears. Things are so well rendered that they seem to come to life. This immerses the reader in a new world, a bubble which blocks out distractions. This is what happens when a reader can't put a book down, when they turn around and hours have passed without them noticing. Because they're so engrossed in the fictive dream that they are entranced.

But how is this achieved? It's about how you describe things, the subject of this chapter. But that is contingent on the POV character and the contract with the reader.

The contract with the reader states a few things about the POV character, as we've discussed. The POV char- acter is the reader, so neither can know any-thing which the other does not know. The POV cannot lie to the reader (unless being an unreliable narrator is part of the story, a rarity). The POV is likely to be the protagonist, the character who is striving toward a goal. While the POV can shift from character to character, a hierarchy should be observed. If the protagonist is in the scene, this is the POV character. This is the reader. But when the protagonist is not in the scene, the character who is striving toward a goal in that scene is the POV charac- ter. This may be the love interest, an ally, even the antagonist. It will be the character who is most impor- tant to the story in that scene.

Whichever character it is, this POV character is the surrogate for the reader. The reader hears what the character hears, sees what the character sees. In fact, this is the crux of the fictive dream; describing every- thing through the sens-es of the POV character. The character sees, hears, tastes, feels, and especially smells things. When the POV character and the reader are strongly bonded, the readers will see, hear, taste, feel, and smell the same things. This is the essence of the fictive dream; it is created in the imagination of the reader, by use of sensory descriptions delivered through the POV character.

Read that sentence again.

This is how you show and not tell, by using sensory description, by exciting the imagination of the reader.

To wit:

> *Jack was nervous. He knew there could be somebody else in that hallway, there had to be. Who else could be making those sounds? He walked slowly toward the door, but his im-agination was filled with terrifying images. He gulped and*

reached for the doorknob.

There's a lot of telling here. I'm telling you Jack is nervous. I'm telling you what he knows. I'm asking a question of the reader, which includes both the reader and the writer in the story (this shatters the fictive dream, because the reader is supposed to be the POV character, not an observer).

Here's another version:

> *Jack's mouth was dry, his heart pounding in his chest. His legs would barely carry him forward, but another thump from behind the door was too much to resist.*
> *Thump, ka-thump. A lump rose in Jack's throat, fingers trembling as they neared the doorknob. Ka-thump.*

Note the difference. I don't use the word nervous, terri- fying, sounds. I present the sounds for the character and the reader to hear. I let the reader feel Jack's dry mouth and pounding heart and trembling fingers, all common symptoms of nervousness and fear. Note that these are feelings; they are sensory. He is hearing, feel- ing, and so the reader is hearing and feeling.

It's especially potent to use the sense of smell, which is most closely associated with memory. Mustiness, urine, body odor, wildflowers, favorite foods, stale tobacco smoke; all these do a lot to characterize a setting or a character, and they do even more to excite the imagination of the reader.

Therefore, you should never use a verb referring to one of these senses. Instead of saying, He *smelled the flowers*, you might write something like *the smell of flowers filled his nostrils*. Instead of He *felt nauseous*, you might write *nauseous bile swirled in his belly*.

Also note that the human brain is powerful, and the reader is an active partner in the reading experience (as we've discussed). Empathize with your reader, as always. Once you lock them to your POV character and use the POV charac- ter's senses to excite the senses and imagination of your reader, know that you don't have to keep doing it over and over again. You don't have to describe every fabric under the POV's fingers, every smell of everything the character comes across. Use these things sparingly. Once the human imagination is set in motion, it only needs to be guided. Sensory descriptions will ignite the imagination, and touch- stone descriptors of the sort will keep the imagination working. At that point, the brain gladly does its part in the storytelling process. You don't have to show every little thing. In fact, that can be tiring to your reader, even exhausting.

This is where the axiom becomes 'show and tell'. Because it's just not practical to use the senses for every description. That much description simply isn't neces- sary, once the brain is fully participating in the story- telling process.

It's about prioritizing. Think of a movie. Every tiny detail isn't shown; it can't be. Only the necessary details are shown. Some are wide angles; they're establishing shots. The closeups are the ones that reveal detail, and those will be telling something important; plot, charac- ter, or theme, for example.

So it is with good writing. Feel free to tell some things, if they are not crucial. Save your showing for the things you need your reader to see, feel, hear, taste, or smell for themselves.

Shattering the Fictive Dream

That's how you induce the fictive dream, but how do you shatter it? Not that you'll want to, of course, but you'll want to know how to avoid doing it accidentally. The fictive dream is a spell, a dream. And in a dream, there is a certain lack of consciousness. If there is a sudden intrusion of consciousness when you're sleeping, you're apt to wake up and whatever dream you were having will be over. So it is with the fictive dream. Sudden bursts of consciousness shatter the dream- world, ending it.

And hard as it is to achieve the fictive dream, shattering it is all too easy and re-establishing it is almost impossi- ble. Once the dream is shattered, the reader is less apt to trust the writer to be able to maintain the dream. The contract with the reader is over and the book is likely never to be finished. So knowing what can shatter the fictive dream is crucial.

In the case of actually sleeping, a sudden burst of consciousness may come from a loud noise in an other- wise quiet room, a thought that is so compelling that it wakes the sleeper, or perhaps some other stimulus. With the fictive dream, that disruption comes from within. The sudden burst of consciousness comes with the raising of questions in the reader's mind. Questions require thought, and that is disruptive of the fictive dream.

Keep in mind that there are two types of questions. Story questions are things the reader asks of him- or herself. They are born of curiosity and engagement in the story: Who is the murderer? Why was the person murdered? Will Brody survive and kill the shark? Will Regan be freed from the demon inside her? Story questions are good; they need to be asked and not answered right away. These are the very reasons people read fiction; the things which, when properly handled, create a page-turning bestseller.

But there are other types of questions, and they are dream-breakers and sto-ry-killers. They are born of disconnection between the reader and story. These are questions that the reader may ask the author. Keep in mind that, as soon as the reader becomes conscious of the writer's presence, the fictive dream is shattered. That is a sudden burst of consciousness, which the deli- cate fictive dream cannot survive. So, when the reader starts asking questions of the writer, there's a real prob- lem. Here they are so you can recognize them later: *What, what, and what?*

But this isn't a case like the one about conflict, conflict, conflict. Here, each 'what' is a different question. Observe:

What's going on? This reader is confused, the action isn't clear.

What are you trying to sell me? This reader isn't convinced. The actions don't fit the characters, the events seem contrived. Things don't happen as they would in the world as we know it. It is not believable, because it is not truthful.

What do I care? This reader isn't seeing the import of what you're presenting, probably because there isn't enough import there. They haven't connected to the characters, they don't relate to their struggle and have no engagement in the outcome.

If the reader asks any one of these questions, the writer has failed and the fictive dream is over, unlikely to return. Never give your readers a chance to ask any one of these three story-killing questions.

Use of Characters

Things can be described, characters in particular, by other characters. We know what we know about people, places, and things, not only from our own experiences but from others. How others react to a stimulus tells us a lot about that stimulus. We see this in the party scene, early on in The Great Gatsby. Gatsby is a mysterious figure, handsome and notorious, which we know by the way his guests speak of him and speculate about his shadowy past.

Characters can describe settings by discussing them, as well. Legends, amulets, and other things are often described by characters, rather than by the author.

Description in Action

Description of an event or character should be marbled into action, not simply dumped at the beginning of the scene. The POV character isn't going to be able to take everything in all at once, and so the reader shouldn't be expected to either. Instead, the details should rise to the fore little by little, as they become relevant. A woman's body may be described in the way she walks, which will also reflect the kind of person she is:

> Her hips swayed, strong thighs flexing as she walked across the room, slow and certain, like a jungle cat closing in for the kill.

Now we know more about her attitude, not just that she's got nice legs.

Combat provides a lot of opportunities for this tech- nique, as do dialogue scenes, where eye contact and little physical mannerisms can be quite telling of the character or the subtext.

Examples

From *A Game of Thrones*

Ser Waymar Royce was the youngest son of an ancient house with too many heirs. [Telling to establish.] He was a handsome youth of eighteen, grey-eyed and graceful and slender as a knife. [Telling to establish.] Mounted on his huge black destrier, the knight towered above Will and Gared on their smaller garrons. [Using description to develop character.] He wore black leather boots, black woolen pants, black moleskin gloves, and a fine supple coat of gleaming black ring- mail over layers of black wool and boiled leather. [Showing.] Ser Waymar had been a Sworn Brother of the Night's Watch for less than half a year, but no one could say he had not prepared for his vocation. At least insofar as his wardrobe was concerned. [Telling.]

His cloak was his crowning glory; sable, thick and black and soft as sin. [Showing.] "Bet he killed them all himself, he did," Gared told the barracks over wine, "twisted their little heads off, our mighty warrior." They had all shared the laugh. [Characters' reactions describe another character.]

From *JAWS*

The fish came closer, silent as a shadow, [using sound] and Hooper drew back. The head was only a few feet from the cage when the fish turned and began to pass before Hooper's eyes – casually, as if in proud display of its incalculable mass and power. [Description to deepen characterization.] The snout passed first, then the jaw, slack and smiling, armed with row upon row of serrate triangles. And then the black, fathomless eye, seemingly riveted upon him. The gills rippled – bloodless wounds in the steely skin. [Description through action.]

Prompts

If you're having trouble showing without telling, think of the game *Taboo*. Pick a celebrity and describe them without using any proper names or titles. How would you describe Albert Einstein or John Lennon? Now describe them only through their settings. Where would you find either man? Make a game of it. Get a partner and see if you can get them to identify the person you're describing, while you use only descrip- tions of their appearance or surroundings.

Exercises

Take a sample of your own writing and circle any words that directly address one of the senses, these words or any conjugations of them: See, hear, taste, touch, smell. Anytime you wrote *see* or *saw*, *hear* or *heard*, and so on, circle it. Now make a list of at least five details, which go along with that verb; in other words, the things the character was hearing or seeing. Let these be vibrant descriptors, active nouns. If it is something visual, include color and texture. If it is sound, include volume or tonal quality.

Another good exercise is to circle emotion words (sad, angry, happy, nervous) and then come up with five vibrant descriptors for how those emotions actually feel. For example, sad might include weak, tired, slug- gish, defeated, alone.

The proper balance of showing and telling will make your setting and characters come alive and create the fictive dream, which will have your readers entranced. Now we move on to another closely related aspect of fiction.

Dialogue.

10

THE VOICES IN THE PAGES

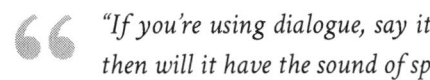 *"If you're using dialogue, say it aloud as you write it. Only then will it have the sound of speech."*

—JOHN STEINBECK (OF MICE AND MEN)

Dialogue is included in just about every piece of longform fiction. In cases of the stage play, dialogue is the primary element of the piece.

Good dialogue performs a lot of story functions, often simultaneously.

They include:

Characterization. How a person speaks and what they say tells us everything about who they are, what they want, and whether they have any chance of getting it. Dialogue is crucial to characterization, because dialogue represents what the character stands for, what their priorities are. And it's not just a matter of what they say, but how they say it. People who are less secure may stutter or stammer. Those who are arrogant will be more grandiose with their statements. A narcissistic character may always include themselves in the context of any conversation, or will say things that reveal the facets of their narcissistic behavior. A very religious person is likely to make biblical references. A person who is drunk may either slur their words or be very careful about overpronouncing them. A person given to profanity is likely to be lowbrow in their upbringing, or they could be fostering anger, bitterness, or disappoint- ment with the world.

Accent is also important to dialogue writing. It's important not to overdo this, however, as it can become a strain on the reader's eyes, to wade through too many apostrophes. Just establish the accent with a turn of phrase and maybe one or two indicators. *Yer* for *your* is effective, so is *ain't* for *isn't*.

Conflict: Dialogue scenes are often rooted in conflict. Lies, cons, negotiations, seductions, manipulations, threats, challenges; all occur in dialogue. And these can be some of the most compelling scenes in fiction. All courtroom dramas turn on compelling cross-examina- tion scenes. All mysteries turn on a reveal in act three, which is almost always presented in dialogue.

Suspense: Suspense presents itself in any number of ways, including visual detail, weather, time (in the form of a looming deadline or *ticking clock*) and in dialogue. But since suspense is literally the forestalling of action, suspense in dialogue is the forestalling of direct communication. So using dialogue to convey suspense is best achieved by using subtext. Prospective lovers might speak of artwork in a particularly sensual way, for example. They might speak of the intercourse of form and function, or the phallic aspects of a tall office building, for example. Two men at odds over a woman may discuss mating rituals in the wild, making thinly veiled threats of violence, as their conflict increases.

Plot: Plot is often furthered in dialogue. Characters discuss the plot often, as a matter of necessity. They have to discuss options, fall back from active scenes to places of consideration, in inactive sequels. It's impor- tant not to let the dialogue carry too much plot infor- mation, which can become exposition. An example of exposition in writing is found in the classic French maid opening of many stage plays. The curtain opens on the setting, often an opulent house, when the phone rings. A girl in a French maid costume enters and answers the phone. She explains to the caller that the man of the house is not at home. She then goes on to explain where he is, what he's been doing, along with the goings-on of other people in the household. This is a way of telling what should be shown; it's just that one character is telling another character, so that the audi- ence can overhear it. Mel Brooks satirizes the conven- tion beautifully in perhaps the funniest moment of his *Star Wars* spoof *Space Balls*. The villainous Dark Helmet trades some information with his lieutenant. He then turns, looks into the camera (at the audience) and asks, "Everybody got that?"

Dialogue can also introduce new information, bringing news to the characters, which changes the plot.

Atmosphere and Mood: These are often well-served by good dialogue. A tense mood is best conveyed by silence, use of short words, extended pauses. A happy atmosphere will have more jokes, people speaking in longer and more fluid sentences, because they feel more at home, more relaxed.

Communicates Theme: Dialogue is great for conveying theme. One character may tell another a story, which echoes the theme. In a telling of the battle of the Alamo, for example, one character may reference the similar battle of Thermo- pylae, which expresses the same theme.

Examples

From *Hills Like White Elephants*

> "Well," the man said, "if you don't want to you don't have to. I wouldn't have you do it if you didn't want to. But I know it's perfectly simple." "And you really want to?"
>
> "I think it's the best thing to do. But I don't want you to do it if you really don't want to."
>
> "And if I do it you'll be happy and things will be like they were and you'll love me?"
>
> "I love you now. You know I love you."
>
> "I know. But if I do it, then it will be nice again if I say things are like white elephants, and you'll like it?"
>
> "I'll love it. I love it now but I just can't think about it. You know how I get when I worry." "If I do it you won't ever worry?"
>
> "I won't worry about that because it's perfectly simple."

Note how the characters come to life; he is dominant, while she is insecure. Note the use of subtext, or symbolism. The actual subject, the termination of her pregnancy (the child is his) is never directly mentioned. Note how the language denotes the time period.

From *Circe*

> "You do not grieve for your father?"
>
> "I do. I grieve that I never met the father everyone told me I had."
>
> I narrowed my eyes. "Explain."
>
> "I am no storyteller."
>
> "I am not asking for a story. You have come to my island. You owe me truth."

A moment passed, and then he nodded. "You will have it."

Note the use of action to replace attribution. Note the tension between the characters, the subtle negotiation, the use of pacing to create suspense.

Tips and Tricks

- Cut the first word of your sentence and see if it doesn't read even better.

- Give every character a different vocal tick. Let one speak only in questions, let one stutter. (But be careful not to overdo this.)

- Let action replace attribution. Instead of writing, *"Get out," he said, lighting a cigarette*, try this: *"Get out." He lit a cigarette.*

- Consider indirect dialogue. Instead of direct question-and-answer patterns, let one character presume the answers. Let one answer questions with questions, or deliberately misdirect the conversation.

- Have characters doing something as they talk; walking, driving, engaging in some physical act. This can add tension and deepen character as well. Remember, it's not just about what they're doing, but how. This reflects mood and atmosphere; if they're doing some mundane chore, like folding laundry, but doing it with unusual tension or fatigue or even delight.

- Get in late, get out early. Keep it short. Enter the conversation at the latest possible point, without the meaning being lost. Get out as soon as you can, to keep the scene from becoming labored or overwrought. This is particularly crucial in dialogue, which can become repetitive.

- Dialogue must either deepen character or further plot. Preferably, it does both.

- Be deliberate with your punctuation. Every pause does not require a comma.

- Read your dialogue out loud to check for flow and realism.

Prompts

If you're having trouble with dialogue, think about the most recent argument you may have had. Who were you arguing with? Over what? What dialogue tech- niques were you unwittingly employing? Misdirection or subtext? How did the argument end? Make a list of the things you find yourself arguing about the most.

Exercises

Watch a silent movie and add dialogue, ignoring the cards inserted by the original filmmakers.

Another good exercise is to find a photograph and create dialogue for it. Naturally, the picture best suited to this exercise will include two or more people, but it could also be someone looking into a mirror or even having a conversation with a dog or other animal, if so pictured. Have fun with it!

Now that you're secure in your use of dialogue, we move forward to the next great aspect of storytelling.

Conflict.

11

CONFLICT IS CRUCIAL

In real estate, there is an old adage about the three most important aspects of a property to consider, when buying. They are 1) location, 2) location, and 3) location. In story, the answer is comparable. What's the most important thing in fiction? 1) Conflict, 2) conflict, and 3) conflict. Conflict is necessary to any story; it's what the story is really all about. Without conflict, there is basically no story at all.

Let's get back to our equation for a good story. We've got our likeable character, and the plot has him or her doing a good deed for others. The equation goes on to specify overwhelming odds.

This is the conflict of the story. Conflict gives the char- acters purpose, urgency; conflict forces unwilling heroes into action. Internal conflict is the principal aspect of the existentialist hero and villain alike.

These odds can take many forms, of course, and there are different types of conflict in fiction.

Classically, there are three types of conflict: Man against man, man against so- ciety, and man against nature. But, as with most things involved in writing, there's more to it than it immediately appears.

First, it's important to note that most stories have more than one type of con- flict. *Moby Dick's* Capt. Ahab is locked in a man against nature struggle, when it comes to his hunt for the white whale. But he is also in conflict with Starbuck, his first mate. And as a man so fixed on revenge, he is in conflict with himself as well. And a lot of stories have characters with both internal (man versus himself) in addition to external conflicts.

Michael Corleone has intense internal conflict, torn between his own desires to be free of his family's crim- inal empire, and his family's need for his proactive participation. He still has plenty of man versus man conflict, as well.

Even so, one type of conflict is likely to dominate a story. In stories like *Moby Dick*, the principal conflict is man against nature.

Other tales of this sort include castaway tales (any telling of Robinson Crusco, or the American film *Cast Away*).

Man versus man stories are often found in Westerns or crime stories, where two characters are positioned to be in direct opposition to one another. *High Noon* is just such a story, as is almost any boxing film, like *Rocky*.

Man versus society is a conflict seen in most rebel or anti-hero tales. This is so, because the anti-hero almost always stands against established society, as in the case of any Robin Hood story. Any parable of the passion of the Christ is also a man-versus-society type story.

And as technology and storytelling have advanced into the modern era, other types of conflict have become so common that they deserve their own place in the classical pantheon.

Man versus technology essentially begins with Mary Shelley's Frankenstein, which has conflicts both internal and external, including man against man (Victor and his creature), man against himself (Victor's ambitions and subsequent guilt), and man against society (the subplot of the wretch and his slow alien- ation from society). But since the wretch (as the crea- ture is often referred to in the novel) is a creation of technology, he is, in a way, a piece of technology himself. And all this, a novel which takes place during the emergence of the sciences in the Enlightenment Period, is essentially the first precautionary tale of tech- nology run amok. Since then, The Strange Case of Dr. Jekyll and Mr. Hyde and a variety of other variations of that tradition have filled bookshelves all over the world. Isaac Asimov's *Robot* series (including *I, Robot*) have kept the tradition alive.

Man against supernatural is another reliable type of conflict, perhaps best typified by William Peter Blatty's *The Exorcist. Rosemary's* Baby was another popular novel, using this type of conflict. These stories often include themes of faith and doubt.

Two other types of conflict are man versus fate and man versus himself. But internal conflict is often used in conjunction with other conflicts. This is the conflicted character we discussed earlier. But this is more the domain of the character than the plot. It's still essential conflict, of course. Think of the novel Sophie's Choice, the story of a woman who must decide which of her children is to be exterminated, or the stage play 'Night, Mother, featuring two characters racked by internal turmoil and hopelessness. Stories of man versus fate are more historical, such as Oedipus Rex, which finds a king doomed by prophecy, who is unable to escape it. One Hundred Years of Solitude has a powerful conflict line of this sort, befitting its core of magical realism.

Tips and Tricks

- Create characters with opposing values, not just opposing goals.

- Create characters with similar values but opposing goals.

- Create characters with different, contrasting personalities, to create conflict.

- Create a powerful antagonist, who will provide overwhelming odds.

- Keep the conflict alive through the long and complex second act.

- Keep smaller conflicts alive (between allies), while pursuing the major conflict.

- Use subplots to maintain conflict.

Prompts

If you're having trouble finding the right conflicts for your story, think again about the last argument you had. What was it about? How did it come about? Is it something that could make a good story, or be in a good story? Think about some of the greatest conflicts you've faced in your life. How did they start? How did you face them, if you ever did?

Exercises

Here are three sentences. This exercise entails creating six sources of conflict for each scenario. So, after the man wins the lottery and before he marries the female bank robber, six challenges or conflicts must occur. They can be any of the types we discussed above.

- A man wins the lottery and marries a female bank robber.

- A woman loses her job and ultimately wins an Olympic gold medal.

- Two people fall in love at a bookstore and later adopt a pet otter.

Now that you've got a good grip on conflict, let's segue into the next significant aspect of storytelling.

12

HOW TO CREATE A PAGE-TURNER

The first book I ever fell in love with was *A Game of Thrones*. I felt transported to a different place, a different time. I found my fictional travel
companions to be new friends and enemies, my new journey a thrilling and
compelling experience. The events seemed to happen right in front of my eyes,
the surroundings coming to life and immersing me in a raucous fictive dream.

For the first time, reading was more than a chore, more than something I had
to do for school. Nothing against *The Great Gatsby*, but there's not much about
the story of 1920s aristocrats embodying the aimless hedonism of the era and
its inherent risks that might amuse a thirteen-year-old boy in the modern era.

After *A Game of Thrones*, I went on to the other books in the series, and then other fantasy books. Time and again, I have been drawn to such books, eager to enter new worlds and to interact with their colorful denizens.

But what makes these books so welcoming, so intrigu- ing? In short, it's a combination of everything we've discussed so far. These books have natural-sounding dialogue, complex characters, vibrant settings, strong story structure. But there's another ingredient, too, some X factor, which only a true page-turner has. What is that X factor? Let's take a closer look at a familiar classic and see if that mysterious facet of fiction reveals itself.

A Game of Thrones

A Game of Thrones and other books in the series remain compulsively readable, perfect examples of a page-turner. It creates the fictive dream and never lets up. Its classic structure holds up and draws the reader along on this incredible journey.

Let's take a more in-depth look at this bestselling page- turner, breaking it down into specific qualities of satis- fying fiction:

Part I: The Prologue

1. Direct POV character experience of dread and fear:

Will could sense something else in the older man. You could taste it; a nervous tension that came perilous close to fear ... Fear filled his gut like a meal he could not digest.

Note the intriguing way the author describes fear as a specific feeling, bringing the action to life.

2. Slanted descriptions, capturing dread and fear:

There was an edge to this darkness that made his hackles rise... A cold wind was blowing out of the north, and it made the trees rustle like living things. All day, Will had felt as though something were watching him, something cold and implacable that loved him not.

Note the use of foreshadowing and the use of senses and setting (the cold of the wind, specifically from the north, the sound of trees rustling).

3. Character conflict:

The young commander is disliked by the men; the conflict starts rising early, to capture the reader's attention.

4. Mystery:

One man finds eight frozen strangers, but the weather has been fair, raising story questions, which keep the reader engaged.

5. Action:

While the book does not start with action, it leads up to it with the whole of the prologue and then delivers at the very end of that small, introductory section. This tells the reader what kind of story they will read, part of the contract with the reader. It also raises more story questions (with the prologue's surprising ending) that will linger in the readers' minds, until they're answered much later in the story.

Part II: Chapter One

A *Game of Thrones'* first chapter begins with a deserter's beheading. The chapter includes all the facets of satisfying fiction:

- Creating Character
- Building the World
- Inciting Incidents (incited by the author)

These incidents include the beheading and the finding of six orphaned wolf pups.

Character development is important here, too. Bran, the chapter's POV character, is a nervous, excited child, even in the face of his father's gruesome behavior on the battlefield. It's a potent set of circumstances for such a young boy.

Bran secures his likeability by doing good deeds for others (saving the orphaned wolf pups). Details are processed through Bran's senses, binding him to the reader.

Martin also prioritizes, showing important things and telling the less important things. Here's how he introduces two non-POV characters, swiftly and clearly, without hampering the reader's attention.

Jon was slender where Robb was muscular, dark where Robb was fair, graceful and quick where his half-brother was strong and fast.

The book goes on from there, and of course, there's no time to analyze the entire book, step by step. These are just a few examples of how Martin created his page- turning bestseller, and how you can use the same devices to have comparable success.

Other Classic Page-turners

It should be no surprise that a lot of the books we've looked at so far are bestsellers, and they're page-turn- ers, too.

JAWS: Primordial terror and relentless suspense put readers on the panicked beaches of Amity, and on the sun-bleached deck of the Orca, in a life-or-death strug- gle, pitting man against nature and against his closest allies.

The Godfather: An epic family tale, which encom- passes generations and even leaves the main family for a significant novel-within-a-novel. But the crisp descriptions and vibrant characters keep the reader involved. A tight bond with the POV protagonist, youngest son Michael, keeps the reader's interest, despite being away from him for significant periods.

Bonfire of the Vanities: I read this 600-page book in two days, with hardly a break. The urgent descriptions, short and pithy, never intrude upon the characters or their conflicts. The scope of the story keeps expanding (in a structure something like a snowflake, with events sprouting from one central event), though the three-act structure is perfectly intact.

The Hobbit: The Middle Earth books are all absorbing to readers, despite their great length, because of their dynamic world-building, sympathetic characters, compelling conflict, and powerful antagonists.

Cliffhangers

The cliffhanger is a narrative device that keeps the character (and the reader) suspended in peril, without resolution. I suggest that every chapter in a page-turner should have a cliffhanger ending, compelling the reader to push on to the next chapter for the resolution.

The term comes from the movie serials of the 1920s, '30s, and '40s. These were long stories (often almost three hours in total), told in installments of fifteen minutes or so. Each chapter followed the derring-do of heroes and heroines and villains. Every installment ended with the hero seeming to meet destruction (often hanging over the edge of a cliff, hence the term). A typical day at the movies would include several of these serial installments, before showing the main attraction (cartoons and news reels were popular parts of the presentation as well). The cliffhanger ending would help bring audiences back the following week.

In the same way, a cliffhanger ending of a chapter keeps the reader coming back for those resolutions. Of course, one resolution is always followed by more action and another cliffhanger ending. Notably, the 1960s campy TV series, Batman, used this device. Unusual for a half-hour show, it showed twice a week, instead of just once. The episodes were written, shot, and presented as two-parters, and the first part always ended with the Dynamic Duo in some sort of cliffhanger situation (usually a death trap of some comedically diabolical sort).

Even the show's hokey, old-fashioned narrator would ramp up the suspense, by asking the viewer what might happen next and extolling them to return two days later, "Same Bat time, same Bat channel."

The cliffhanger is commonly used in film today, thanks in part to the popularity of film franchises. It's very common for a film in any comic book movie franchise (DC or Marvel), or series such as the Monsterverse films, which gave us Godzilla's recent screen outings, to end with a teaser for the next movie. This is a callback to the cliffhanger endings of old, a way to keep the viewers wondering what was coming next, already securing their willingness to return and see more.

We've seen how story structure works, and briefly how scene structure works. But we now must take a closer look at scenes and sequels, to see how a real page- turner works.

There are ten different types of cliffhangers:

- An Unanswered Question: Increases suspense and raises the stakes; how high depends on the answer.

- A Loss: Raises the stakes for sufferers of the loss and provides story twists and new motivations.

- A Possible Reward: Raises the stakes.

- A New Hope: Raises the stakes.

- A Physical Threat: Increases the conflict.

- Foreboding and Foreshadowing: Increases suspense.

- A Ticking Clock: Increases urgency and raises the stakes.

- An Accident: Increases the conflict and provides story twists.

- Unexpected News: Increases the conflict and provides story twists.

- An Unmade Decision: Increases suspense and raises the stakes; how high depends on the decision.

Scene and Sequel Structure

We've touched on this briefly, as it relates to protago- nists. Every protagonist strives for something, both in the story as a whole and in every scene. Every scene goal will intend to bring the protagonist one step closer to achieving the main story goal. But every scene will also present significant conflict, which should result in a setback, or disaster. This unit of drama is called the scene: Goal, conflict, disaster.

This often leads a character to react, reconsider, and embark on a new course of action. This unit of drama is called the sequel: Emotion, thought, decision.

The only other unit of drama is the transition, which links scenes and sequels, as necessary, to advance time or place. But scenes and sequels are where the story is told.

The scene, which begins with a goal and includes conflict, ends in disaster for the scene protagonist. But there are four distinct types of disasters or outcomes, answers to the protagonist's efforts toward the scene goal. These are:

- Yes
- No
- Yes, but ...
- No, and furthermore ...

A *yes* answer or disaster gives the protagonist what they wanted at the begin- ning of the scene, despite the conflict. This is the weakest answer, from a dra- matic perspective. The conflict doesn't rise, nor do the stakes. The protagonist is better off than before.

A *no* answer is better. The protagonist's efforts are of no use and another, prob- ably more dangerous, course of action must be pursued. This is better than yes, as it further challenges the character and, thus, the reader. It's still not that strong, because the character is no better off, but he or she is no worse off, either.

Yes, but ... is stronger still. Here we have irony, compli- cation and elevated conflict. *Yes*, the character gets what they want, *but* there is an unexpected complication that makes things even harder for the protagonist. In some ways, the character is worse off than before.

No, and furthermore ... is the strongest dramatic outcome for a scene. This provides plot twists, raised conflicts, higher stakes, and suspense. Not only does the char- acter not get what they want, but they are also worse off than before.

A real page-turner observes scene and sequel structure. A real page-turner has *no, and furthermore ...* scene endings, which keep the protagonist scrambling against ever-increasing odds, ever-rising conflicts. A real page- turner uses sequels sparingly, never using two sequels in a row. A real page-turner uses those sequels to increase inter-character conflict and deepen characterization.

It's the right scene structure (with proper *no, and furthermore ...* endings) and balance of scene-to-sequel that keeps a story moving forward through its three acts. And this is the key to bringing the reader along on that long and often complicated journey.

Here are some examples of proper scene and sequel structure:

In the film version of JAWS, Quint's goal is to draw the shark into the shallow waters and drown it. He states this clearly. The conflict comes when the shark chases the Orca, causing Quint to burn out the engine. The disaster is clear: No, Quint did not manage to draw the shark in and drown it as intended, *and furthermore* the Orca is now stranded and helpless.

Next, we see a sequel, where the characters react to the previous action. The first thing we see is emotion; Hooper is clearly frightened, Brody is confused, Quint is defeated. Next we *see thought*; Quint looks around his battered ship, seeing that all his weaponry has failed against the shark. The only thing he has left to offer is a pair of life jackets. He asks Hooper what he can do with the spear and cage. Hooper explains his desperate plan to take the cage into the water and poison the shark, in hand-to-hand combat. Brody urges him against the move as near-suicide, but they have no choice. Their *decision* is made.

This leads them into the next scene. Hooper's goal is to go down in the cage and poison the shark, as stated in the previous sequel. The conflict is that the shark tears the cage apart and Hooper winds up unarmed, pinned to the ocean floor. The disaster is that no, Hooper failed to kill the shark, and furthermore he is now helpless. If the other two men don't kill that shark, the shark will get Hooper, as well. In the book, Hooper is taken by the shark, in a no, and further-more … ending that is even worse for the young oceanographer.

Observe scene and sequel structure and keep the conflict high, by offering your characters *no, and furthermore* … whenever you can, and your readers will keep turning those pages.

Tips and Tricks

- Plan plot twists: A linear plot is boring. Include plot twists that even you, the writer, don't expect. This is why a flexible outline is so crucial, so both the reader and writer can be suitably surprised.

- Use subplots to provide plot twists: This is largely what a good subplot is for, to influence the main plot.

- Introduce a ticking clock: This generates new urgency and suspense, crucial to a page- turner.

- End every chapter should end on a cliff-hanger: Never resolve anything in a chapter. Always forestall any resolution. End the chapter at a point where the reader can least afford to walk away.

- Raise the stakes: Continuously give your protagonists more to lose. Let every goal set them back even further.

- Create quirky, unpredictable characters (as they do quirky, unpredict-able things).

- Increase the obstacles too: How do the stakes get raised? Introduce big-ger obstacles, odds that are even more overwhelming.

- Use irony: It surprises the characters and the reader, as well, and keeps them all involved in the story.

- Create a conflicted antagonist: The more compelling the antagonist, the more compelling the story.

- Use detail to bring the fictive dream to life.

- Use red herrings to keep the readers guessing: There's nothing more boring than predictability, especially in fiction. Red herrings deliberately misdirect the reader's attention, keeping them guessing and keeping them reading.

- Use character backstory: This adds depth to the action and to the character. This is where the seeds of irony are planted, to be harvested later in the plot.

- Use short words, sentences, and paragraphs: That keeps the read fast and tight.

- Don't overdo it on description. If you're properly appealing to the senses, a little will go a long way.

- Shifting viewpoints will keep the reader engaged over the long haul and will give greater life to more characters.

- End chapters in the middle of a scene. A great spot is just after the conflict and just before the disaster, or just after the goal and right before the conflict begins. These are the moments of greatest tension in a scene.

Prompts

If you're having trouble making sure your book is a page-turner, think about the books you loved reading. Pick them up and read them again, just for a scene or two. What do your favorite authors do? Use those tech- niques yourself; there's nothing wrong with that. The old axiom is this: *Good artists borrow, but great artists steal.*

Here's another: Do you remember the old Batman show? Try to think back to as many death traps as you can. You won't use any of them, but it should get your cliffhanger juices flowing. Some of them were quite creative and amusing.

Exercises

Cliffhangers are often used before commercial breaks on television. So, watch a TV show (either a half-hour sitcom or an hour-long drama) and outline it as it happens. Note what is an action-driven scene or a reac- tion-driven sequel. Note the goal, conflict, and disaster of each scene; also the emotion, thought, and decision of each sequel. Note where the commercial breaks happen, and what cliffhangers are presented at those points (there *will* be cliffhangers there, I assure you). Soap operas are perfect for this exercise. Note: Make sure to use broadcast episodes or basic cable shows, which break for commercials. An hour-long episode of anything on HBO won't have the same act breaks or cliff-hangers.

Now that you've got a page-turning potential bestseller, filled with strong scenes and sequels that push your characters and readers through the story, with plenty of cliffhangers to keep the pages turning, let's turn our attention to the next crucial aspect of good fiction.

Rereading and editing.

13

REREADING, EDITING ...
AND WHEN TO STOP

It has a lot of unpleasant connotations, doesn't it? But it's a necessary part of writing, and it's more than just making corrections. Editing involved a family of behaviors, really, broken down into three major groups:

- Content Editing
- Line Editing
- Proofreading

They're in this order for a reason, from macro to micro.

Content editing includes the big stuff: Story and scene structure, character motivations, consistency of the setting, plot holes (more on these in a moment). This is where you may have to reconsider your characters, your significant beats, motivations and other complexi- ties. This is where you may find your characters or plots or settings lacking in uniqueness, significance, adequate quirkiness or likeability. You might find the dreaded what questions leaking in at this stage. This is when the writer has to be open-minded and open- hearted enough to reconsider their original impulses, to redream the dream.

Line editing brings us to the more specific: Sentence structure, dialogue, smoothness of the prose, the rhythm of the prose; these are the concerns of line edit- ing. Is the dialogue unique to each character and true to each character? Does the prose match the content? Is your prose translucent and not transparent?

Proofreading is the art of finding technical mistakes. This can be hardest for the writer to accomplish, because the writer's brain fixes those mistakes subconsciously. Here is where repeated words, syntax, and punctuation are straightened out.

Plot Holes

These happen, even in the best-plotted stories. One may discover later that there are logical inconsisten- cies, which need to be quickly explained, but for some reason can't be. The danger here is that readers notice them and, when they do, that shatters the fictive dream. This is where any one of the dreaded story- killing what questions may arise. Readers fall through them and out of the dream, because of the sudden burst of consciousness they get from their confusion or their disbelief or even their impatience. For exam- ple, explaining something in great detail, simply to explain something else later, will tire your reader, testing their patience. You won't be there to reassure them that the information will be handy later. If you need that information, put it in. But there's a quicker and easier way to do it, and that's to hang a lantern on it.

This phrase comes from the problem: Instead of filling a hole in a mine, workers would hang a lantern over it, so others would see it, be aware of it, and move on. Plot holes in story do the same thing.

Here are a few common plot holes and the lanterns you can hang to remedy them:

- Behavioral inconsistency in a character: Sometimes people just snap. Panic brings out our worst.

- Misplaced object: People can lose track of things in a chaotic situation.

- Inconsistency of time: People can lose track of time in a chaotic situation.

Basically, inconsistency is often at the root of a plot hole. So, embracing the natural inconsistencies of life is a good way to get through them. Don't let this happen too often, though. It's lazy writing, the reader will notice all those lanterns and you will lose their trust and confidence.

When to Start

You have to reread your book, at least once (and perhaps dozens of times). That's why you have to write what you like, what you believe in, because you may have to read it over ... and over ... and over again.

First, before you start rereading and rewriting, get away from the book for a while. Cleanse your mind of it. Give your imagination time to wander to other areas, other things. Spend time with your friends and family. After the countless hours (or perhaps you did count them) of writing, you may owe some people a little extra attention. You may be one of those people yourself. Hours of sitting and typing may have allowed a few extra pounds to collect here, a few inches to disappear there. Spend some time working out, going out, doing or thinking about anything other than your book, or even about writing in general.

This is important, for physiological reasons as much as for social. First of all, you don't want to become myopic. There's more to life than writing, and it does go by quickly. Variety is, after all, the spice of life.

Most importantly, this is about the human brain and how it functions. The brain is divided into two hemi- spheres. The right hemisphere is dedicated to creative pursuits, while the left specializes in analytical think- ing. People generally use both, but at different times.

But what people often don't realize is that the brain doesn't switch quickly from one side to another. It takes a while, depending on how long one side has been used. The longer you're relying on one side of the brain, the longer the adequate transfer time from one hemi- sphere to the other.

This is why some people consider themselves naturally more left-brained or right-brained. But the truth is, that everybody has more or less equal capacity on both sides. But some people, writers for example, spend so much time using the creative right hemisphere that they rarely switch over to left-brain analytics. They don't consider transfer time. Switching from months of right-brain creativity, suddenly to left-brain analytics, can make it feel as if the switch isn't possible at all. It is, it just takes time.

The brain is so powerful, this phenomenon so perva- sive, that some people believe that no writer can adequately reread their own work. I don't agree. But there are physiological aspects to this that must be considered.

Regardless of the brain hemispheres, and there's really no getting around them, there is also the question, not of what the brain is or how it works, but whose brain it is. In a normal reader situation, the reader has no preconception of what it is seeing. It's like seeing it for the very first time (which, more often than not, is precisely what's happening). The eye is telling the brain what it is seeing. Even this has its limitations, but it is more or less the dynamic at play.

But when the writer reads his or her own work, the brain does have a precon- ception of what it is seeing. In this case, the brain tells the eye what it expects to see, and will recognize what it chooses to recognize, not what the eye dictates. In this case, the brain is telling the eye what it is seeing, and not the other way around.

So, the writer needs an extraordinary amount of time away from the piece, just to be in consideration for reading it with an editor's eye. Even then, memory tells the eye what the brain wants to see. This is why it's so crucial to get feedback from others and to always have somebody else proofread the work. The internet has made finding proofreaders easier (but a bit pricier) than ever.

When to Stop

This can be harder than you think. After all the years you spent thinking about writing, years studying books and stories, then months or perhaps years planning and then writing your first novel. You then invested even more time and care rereading, reconsidering every aspect, both great and small. You may have formed an attachment to the piece, as if it were your own child. You may be hesitant to send that child out into the cold, cruel world.

You may be inclined to second-guess yourself. Would one more pass make it better? Are there still one or two mistakes lingering in the text?

Congratulations, *now* you're a writer!

Another old axiom (I like them, as you can tell) is that you can never really finish a piece of art, you can only abandon it. Consider the great Leonardo Da Vinci, perhaps the world's greatest artistic mind. He was infa- mous for not finishing his projects. Sometimes they were cut short by circumstance, sometimes he lost interest. But often enough, he just couldn't stop work- ing. He held onto his *Mona Lisa* for a decade or so after it was commissioned, dragging it around and working on it, little by little, until he finally had no choice but to surrender it to his patron.

At some point, you're only switching words around, replacing one with another and then back again. At some point, you're only mucking around with it and not improving it. At some point, you're going to be nauseated by the sight of the damn thing.

Hopefully.

This brings us to the notion of perfectionism, which can be a crippling condition. It causes procrastination, preventing finishing or even beginning projects. It causes overthinking, the psychological tendency to endlessly imagine one or both of two things; how events might have gone differently in the past, or how they might occur in the future. But since the past cannot be changed and the future cannot be predicted or controlled, overthinking is a folly. It also contributes to a fixed mindset, one which holds that outcomes are predestined, that a loser is a loser and a winner is a winner. This is antithetical to a writer's viewpoint, which should hold a growth mindset and believe that failure is part of the process of success, that potential remains in everyone (and in every character).

If you are to be a good writer (and a well-adjusted person), you must abandon perfectionism. Nothing and nobody will ever be perfect. Perfection is subjective, and writers and other artists evolve (the good ones do). So what is perfect to the artist in his or her twenties will likely fall far short of perfection in retrospect, ten years down the road. Perfection is subjective and illusory.

So, the important thing is to do your best, write to your maximum capacity. Another old axiom: Always do your best. It's all you can do, and all anybody can ever ask of you. And once you've done your best, move on to the next project. That is the measure of your success as an artist.

You will make mistakes and learn lessons. That is a part of the process. And the only way to really make these mistakes and learn these lessons is to do it, as we agreed early on. That means doing it again, and again, and again. Think of your favorite authors; were they one- hit wonders, or writers of several books, authors of a canon, not merely a book?

Read Like A Reader

Before, I told you that, to be a writer, you'd have to learn to read like a writer. You have to have an eye for techniques, the critical eye of the editor, and these are things readers simply don't have to worry about. They get to let the story wash over them, to indulge in that wondrous fictive dream.

When you begin to reread your own work, you'll be compelled to read like a writer, an editor. You'll find it hard not to. But you'll have to be deliberate about it. The first time you read it, don't make notes. Just read, just let the story wash over you. You have to read it as a reader would.

What's worse, once you've read it like a reader, you'll have to go back and read it again, this time like a writer. Hey, nobody ever said it was going to be easy.

Beware of Redundancies

Redundancies are the most common form of bad writ- ing. Redundancies can be explicit, as when a word is reused too often (*Jack was very tall, with a very handsome face*) or if a line of dialogue is basically repeated, without adding anything new (*"What do you want? What are you doing here?"*). Redundancies can also be implied (*He looked at the sky above*, but where else would the sky be?) This can happen in the macro, with superfluous characters or events, or in the micro, as in with repeated words or needless repetition.

Tips and Tricks

Here are some ways to make sure your editing is as effi- cient as possible:

- Print it out: It's better for the eyes and you can write down notes where appropriate.

- Read it out loud: It forces your eye to be more precise and gives you a feel for readability.

- Make notes: Don't think about them, just scribble and keep reading.

- Make changes: Identify common mistakes and do a document search for them.

- Read your manuscript backwards, sentence by sentence, to force the eyes to overcome the brain's prejudices.

Prompts

Having trouble with your editing? Find something online to read; it doesn't matter what it is. Read it and edit it. You'll find mistakes, repetitions, all kinds of things to get your editing blood pumping.

Exercises

Here are ten good editing exercises:

- Go through your manuscript for repeated words. Most word programs will count how many times a word occurs. Conjugations of the verbs *to say* or *to be* don't really count, as they are essentially invisible to the human eye. Look for names being repeated too often, especially in a single sentence.

- Track your readability score, using online sites, such as analyzemywriting.com.

- Check your manuscript for adverbs (they usually end in ly). Replace as many as you can with short, active verbs.

- Search for long sentences and cut them into two short sentences.

- Search for slang or cliches and cut every one of them.

- Rewrite your biography for the book.

- Write a sonnet or a haiku, to help you think like an editor.

- Write a flash fiction story (from 100 to 1,000 words), to help you think like an editor.

- Search for 'and' in your manuscript and question the use every time.

- Pretend you're paying yourself a dime for every word cut, then cut as much as you can from one sample chapter of your book.

A big part of editing is feedback, so let's take a closer look at that in the next chapter.

14

THE VALUE OF INPUT

"Writer friends are everything! We all know that the act of novel writing is solitary, and some- times lonesome work, but when you crawl out of your cave it's so important to have friends there waiting who get it, who are ready to read and cheer you on, and who will send you right back into the cave when you need it."

— AFIA ATAKORA (CONJURE WOMEN)

The first time I joined an informal writing group, I was nervous. I liked my book well enough, but that wasn't a guarantee of anything. I was nervous and presumptuous. I didn't much like some of the other writers' work, though I did find one or two to be excep- tional. I was quietly judgmental and I assumed everyone else was, too, at least at first.

But the nervousness slipped away pretty quickly and I found the experience beyond educational. I learned a lot about my book, to be sure, and my writing in general. I definitely came out of it a better writer and even a better person. Because I learned just as much about myself as I did about my writing. I learned that I was more average in some ways than I thought, and more above average than I thought in other ways. I was more resilient than I expected, and the criticism didn't hurt nearly as much as I thought it would. Plus, I made some good friends and had a good time, which can be hard enough these days, especially for a writer.

Once you've decided to step away from the book, know that you may yet return to it. But before you do, it's time to get some feedback. This can be intim- idating, even frightening, and it's where a lot of projects fall apart. A writer may become disillu- sioned by others' reactions, or by their criticism. They may not know how to take a note, which is shorthand for understanding that giving and taking notes both have their delicacies and pitfalls, as we'll soon see.

Hell, let's do it right now.

When giving notes:

- First, be positive: Point out what you liked about the piece.

- Second, be fair: Admit that everything is subjective. Instead of pointing out shortcomings or failings, say only that other decisions might yield even stronger dramatic returns. It's not about assaulting the writer, but improving the book.

- Third, be calm: Emotion and reason cannot coexist in the same mind at the same time. Keep emotion out of it, especially since the writer may become emotional.

- Fourth, do not attack: The writer will be defensive. Don't put the writer in the line of fire, only the work.

- Fifth, provide alternatives: Don't just say what you don't like, offer alternatives that may work better or at least will illustrate your point.

- Sixth, be gracious: If the writer doesn't take the notes, that's their loss, not yours. Don't push it.

When getting notes:

- First, do not be defensive: Close as you may feel to the work, this isn't about you, it's about the work, and they are different things. Nobody gets it right the first time.

- Second, be fair: You're putting somebody in a tight spot, if they don't like the work. Be empathetic with them about that.

- Third, be calm: Emotion and reason cannot coexist in the same mind at the same time. Do not let yourself become emotional. Stay reasonable.

- Fourth, do not defend: Don't defend yourself or the work. The reader understands what you intended, they just read the book. But their opinions differ in some way, and you're involved in the feedback process to get those opinions. Take them. You don't have to agree or incorporate them into your writing; just be openhearted and open-minded.

- Fifth, don't decide then and there: It's best to take notes without argument, digest them over the course of a day or two, or even longer, then decide which notes to use and which to reject.

- Sixth, ask questions if you're confused or would like to hear more suggestions or alternatives, or even to brainstorm.

Some feedback is useful, some not. You may simply disagree; just make sure you give every bit of criticism the right amount of fair consideration. Some people will just have wildly different tastes than you do. Here's where subjectivity is so important. Also, consider the source when getting feedback. Some people are going to have ulterior motives and hang-ups of their own.

You'll be facing some of your deepest and darkest fears, when seeking feedback for your work. So understand that, give yourself a slight margin for your discomfort and then a pat on the back for facing your fears. Then do it.

But good feedback, well-taken, can have immeasurable benefits for your book and for your writing. You can learn things no book can teach you. You can get fresh insights into your book, your plot and characters and setting, which you may not be able to get anywhere else. You'll get an insight into what even the most skep- tical reader may say. You will learn to externalize your- self from your work, which is something only a person with a true growth mindset can do. You will learn to abandon the narcissism of perfectionism and learn that, sadly, you are not right about everything all the time. You will meet other writ- ers and give them your own feedback, as well. You'll learn lessons from their writ- ing, which you can apply to your own. You may even find a romance worth writing a book about! This won't work out, if you're just having your family members read the book, of course.

That's probably not even the best way to go, if you want real feedback. Family is biased and dishonest in all kinds of ways. Even your friends are apt to be more kind than constructive, and in truth, you're imposing on them, to have them read a whole novel (unless they're truly begging for it).

A good way is to join a workshop or class, of which there are dozens readily available, both in person or online. It will seem daunting, because it is daunting. But it's a rite of passage for writers, as well, and if you don't have writers in your family (and even if you do), going to eager outsiders is a risk worth taking.

Workshop or Class?

Which is best for you, a class or a workshop? Let's compare them to find out.

Classes have less participation than workshops; you're more apt to listen and learn than get any real work done on your book. If you're shaky on the basics, a class might be best; or if you're looking to write in a very specific genre. If you're insecure or wish to be private about your writing, a class is probably best. Classes rely more on the instructor.

Workshops are more participatory and rely more on the writers than the instructor. If you're tough enough to have other people really muck around with your work, going so far as to make suggestions for changes, you may be ready for a workshop.

Competitions and Submissions

This is another way to get feedback, but of course the bar of judgment will be set a lot higher. You're competing with more accomplished writers and in front of judges, with less patience for weak writing. You may get feedback, but it may just be a rejection, or it may not be as empathetic as you'd like.

There are numerous writing competitions online, but do your due diligence. A lot of them are hucksters, just trying to take your money. Some legit contests will have fees, however. You'll have to do your research, to discover which competitions are worth your time and money and which ones aren't.

If you're a screenwriter and you're submitting your script, be careful. Screenplays get notes known as coverage, and once this happens, your script will likely never be read, only the coverage will. That means the first person's opinion of your script will basically be everybody's opinion of it, as that's all they'll ever read.

Like classes and goals (or even more so), submissions to competitions can give you an impetus to finish the work, a deadline you have to meet. That can reinvigo- rate your sense of drive and refresh your excitement about the project. You may also find an audience, make valuable connections, and build your reputation.

You can also submit articles to magazines and journals (most likely for their online iteration). You'll get plenty of feedback here, if you're ready for it. Make sure your work is edited and of professional quality before you submit to a magazine like *The New Yorker*, or newspapers like *The New York Times*.

And you may pick up a few bucks from any of these submissions. You may also pick up a few bruises to your ego.

Prompts

If you're having trouble dealing with feedback, think of it not as an attack or even as being about the work. Imagine every note is a green vegetable. It's not about you; nobody likes broccoli! But it's still good for you and you should take your portion when it comes around. It's good for you, and with a little cheese, it's really not so bad.

Exercises

Make a list of competitions where you might submit your work. Arrange them by deadline and schedule your submissions. Some will want excerpts of varying lengths, some the entire book. This will give you time to perfect your submissions.

Well, that pretty much brings us to the end of our jour- ney. You began at the inception of the idea, developed the story, staked out places and times to write, and then set about doing it. You discovered what made for compelling stories, unforgettable characters, and enduring settings, to create a page-turning potential bestseller.

But let's not presume to have the final word on things. I humbly suggest we turn things over to the great figures of our craft and learn from them directly, by taking advice from the masters.

Leave a 1-Click Review

If you like this book, please leave a review. Scan the QR code below to be taken directly to the review page!

CONCLUSION

Congratulations. You have come to the end of this journey. You are now a writer. You have researched and reviewed your influences. You have mastered the ancient secrets of structure and character and dialogue. You have learned to decode the mysteries of setting and scene and sequel, theme and pacing. You have plumbed a treasure trove of pearls from the world's, indeed from history's, greatest artists.

Whoever you are and wherever you are on your writer's journey, this leg of it has come to an end. But if we learned anything from A Game of Thrones and countless other classics, it's that every ending is a new beginning. The lessons you've learned here will stay with you into the rest of your writing career and of your life. Even if you never write another word in your life, you have scaled the mountain and taken up the challenge that most run from. You stayed the course where most others gave up. You finished where few people do, and pushed your vision out into the world.

Or you may turn back and take another writer's jour- ney. You'll find the next book comes even more smoothly. You'll find yourself innovating techniques to match particular challenges, techniques you can call your own. Your writing will take on its own style, your stories will inspire and impress and delight. You now have the confidence to make time enough to meet any challenge, whatever it is.

If you keep writing, you may find yourself continuing to study as well. There are other books like this one, many from our own catalogue. They will take you into the furthest reaches of fiction, broadening your hori- zons beyond your wildest dreams. We urge to go on with your studies, your journeys, your dreams. And we want to be there with you every step of the way, on the first read or the tenth, on this subject and an array of others.

If you enjoyed this book; if it's made you feel that you can overcome any challenge, if it's helped you produce a book that you're proud of, if it's helped you secure a growth mindset over a fixed mindset, then it's more than done its job. We're happy to oblige. If you take a little time to share the book's benefits with a good review on Amazon, that would help others face the same challenges you have mastered. And it would help us to go on producing books like this, helping you and people just like you!

Keep reading, keep writing, keep living!

Want more?

As you close this book, don't let the adventure end. Scan the QR code below to unlock a treasure trove of insights from the second book in the Fiction 101 series. "A Guide to Crafting Compelling Characters" isn't merely a book; it's a toolbox, brimming with essential elements for crafting characters and narratives that captivate readers. Elevate your storytelling prowess and embark on a transformative journey in the realm of fiction.

Fiction writing 101:
A Guide to Crafting
Compelling
Characters

If you are interested in more tips, tricks, and exercises as well as some great memes related to fiction writing, you can always join our Facebook group.

Simple scan the QR code to join today!

Free gift just for you!

An Insiders Tips to Better Dialogue

Thank you for choosing this book. As a token of our appreciation, we are giving you a small gift as part of your purchase.

Simply scan the QR code to receive it today!

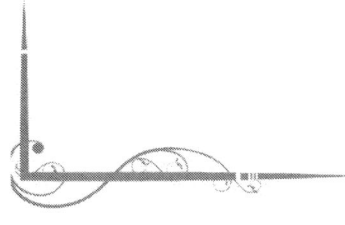
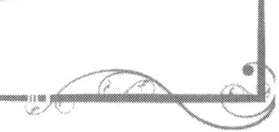

REFERENCE LIST

Benchley, P. (1974). Jaws. Doubleday.

Bingham, H. (2020). *Write your Novel with the Snowflake Method (Simple Example)*. [online] Jericho Writers. Available at: https://jerichowrit ers.com/how-to-plot/ [Accessed 1 Nov. 2022].

Bunting, J. (2020). *Freytag's Pyramid: Definition, Examples, and How to Use this Dramatic Structure in Your Writing*. [online] The Write Practice. Available at: https://thewritepractice.com/freytags-pyramid/ .

Clark, C. (2018). *25 Writing Tips From Famous Writers*. [online] Freewrite Store. Available at: https://getfreewrite.com/blogs/writing- success/writing-tips-from-famous-writers .

Ehiosun, J. (2022). *A Game of Thrones Plot Summary*. [online] Book Analysis. Available at: https://bookanalysis.com/george-r-r- martin/a-games-of-thrones/summary/ [Accessed 1 Nov. 2022].

Gilbo, S. (n.d.). *How to Outline Your Novel with the Save the Cat! Beat Sheet*. [online] www.savannahgilbo.com. Available at: https://www. savannahgilbo.com/blog/plotting-save-the-cat [Accessed 1 Nov. 2022].

Goodreads.com. (2011). *Writing Quotes (12131 quotes)*. [online] Available at: https://www.goodreads.com/quotes/tag/writing .

Hemingway, E. (1927). *Hills Like White Elephants*. Men Without Women.

Jaws. (1975). Universal Pictures.

Jenkins, J. (2019). *7 Story Structures Any Writer Can Use*. [online] Jerry Jenkins | Proven Writing Tips. Available at: https://jerryjenkins. com/story-structures/

Lapena, S. (2016). *Top Ten Tips for Writing a Page-Turner - Strand Magazine.* [online] Strand Mag. Available at: https://strandmag. com/top-ten-tips-for-writing-a-page-turner/ .

Majewski, J. (2021). *Plotter vs. Pantser: What Are You?* [online] whenyouwrite. Available at: https://whenyouwrite.com/plotter-vs- pantser/ [Accessed 1 Nov. 2022].

Martin, G.R.R. (2017). *A game of thrones.* New York: Bantam Books, [Geschat.

Miller, M. (2019). *Circe.* Bloomsbury publishing.

Puzo, M. (1969). *The Godfather.* G. P. Putnam's Sons.

Rexford, S. (2022). *Fichtean Curve Story Structure.* [online] self-publishingschool.com. Available at: https://self-publishingschool.com/ fichtean-curve-story-structure/ [Accessed 1 Nov. 2022].

Scroggs, L. (2022). *The Pomodoro Technique – Why It Works & How To Do It.* [online] Todoist. Available at: https://todoist.com/productivity- methods/pomodoro-technique [Accessed 1 Nov. 2022].

Studiobinder (2020). *How Dan Harmon's Story Circle Can Make Your Story Better.* [online] StudioBinder. Available at: https://www. studiobinder.com/blog/dan-harmon-story-circle/ .

The Godfather. (1972). Paramount Pictures.

THE WIZARD OF OZ (1939). Loew's, Inc.

Young, J. (2020). *Researcher Behind '10,000-Hour Rule' Says Good Teaching Matters, Not Just Practice - EdSurge News.* [online] EdSurge. Available at: https://www.edsurge.com/news/2020-05-05-researcher- behind-10-000-hour-rule-says-good-teaching-matters-not-just- practice [Accessed 1 Nov. 2022].

Printed in Great Britain
by Amazon

55900550R00079